A GUNNER'S VOW
I wished to be a pilot
And you along with me.
But if we all were pilots
Where would the Air Force be?
It takes GUTS to be a Gunner.
To sit out in the tail
When the Messerschmitts are coming
And the slugs begin to wail.
The pilot's just a chauffeur.
It's his job to fly the plane;
But it's We who do the fighting,
Though we may not get the fame.
If we all must be Gunners
Then let us make this bet;
We'll be the best damn Gunners
That have
STARS AND STRIPES WEE
Bridge Blasted
Mitchells Range
ver Brenner Pass
F HQ., March 30—The Bat-
Brenner Pass continued to-
ith planes of the 12th AAF
in for the first time in four
reports from the day's op-
revealed that B-25 Mit-
ad again attacked the im-
rail bridge at San Ambro-
the Brenner rail line 12
rth of Verona. This was
nd time in two days that
ge had been attacked by
ctical planes.
Brenner attacks fol-
ay during which MATAF
w more than 900 sorties,
and strafing enemy sup-
llations, communications,
d, and front-line strong-
northern Italy and Yugo-
Brenner attacks yester-
22nd Tactical Air Com-
red direct hits on the
avis rail bridges, and at-
idges and fills at San
Ala, Rovereto and San
tailed results of today's
Brenner were still un-
MAAF reported that
hunderbolts on missions
Italy had destroyed 20
th of Novara, had suc-
ackrd ammunition
in the Spezi
1945
Four Lile Boys Now In
Service, Mother Says
Four sons of Mr. and Mrs. H. D.
Lile of Columbia, S. D., but former-
ndale are now in the
s, the latter informed
his week. Keith is a
the 12th air force
sle of Corsica, Wen-
orce training center
versity, Calif., Bob
pany in the South
with the signal
wder, Mo.
Roy is working
et Sound and
pper, a very exacting
the Tacoma, Wash., ship-
Mr. Lile is
Peaches in Miami Beach, Florida
BUNNY AND EASTE
HAPPY EAST
FRITZ!
Instructio

To my flight crew,
Haley, Krister, and Dylan
and to
Lana, Keegan, and Riley
for keeping me going

Let's do this thing!

Thanks,
S

S.T. LILE

THE TAIL GUNNER

BERING STREET BOOKS

Gig Harbor, Washington

Library of Congress Cataloging-in-Publication Data is available.
ISBN 978-0-9896505-0-2

10 9 8 7 6 5 4 3 2 1
Printed in the United States of America
First edition, November 2014

Fonts used for this book include Hoefler, Minion, Palatino
and American Typewriter.
Cover photograph courtesy of the KBL Family Collection.
Book design by Phyllis Bartling and Steve Alexander of
Futura Design, Shelburne, Vermont.

Contents

CHAPTER ONE

THE RED DIARY

Everyone has secrets. Even if we forget their exact origin, we haul them around from year to year, burying them deeper and deeper until we have no idea where they are or how they came to make us. Are they really our own, or did we borrow them from someone else to make our lives glimmer with mysterious or marvelous depth? When we die and someone else finds them, are they secrets still? And when they pile so high and so heavy that they crush the very memories they were meant to protect, do they even matter anymore? Grandma once told me that secrets were like wet sheets—you had to hang them out on a clothesline so they didn't mold in a dark, damp heap. But when I unearthed her secrets one drippy-cold day on our last summer at the farm, hanging them out in the open was the last thing she wanted. If she'd had her way, the whole lot of them would have been burned.

As for me, the only secrets I thought I had that summer were a graduation adventure to Alaska with my best friend Penelope and the bad poetry in my art journal. But all that went to hell when bomber boy Bish showed up demanding my help. Never in a million years would I have guessed that I'd be the one to see ghosts. Supernatural stuff was Pen's thing. I wanted to be an artist, even though Mom said I'd starve.

That summer began just like the sixteen summers before, with Mom running around like a well-polished freak, trying to hide her excitement about flying off to Europe while getting me "settled" with Grams and Grandpa Chuck. But now that Grandpa Chuck was gone, everything seemed hollow and fake.

"Sylvie, let's go." Mom grabbed my wheeliebag and headed for the door of our condo. "Motivate, levitate, and stop that scribbling, for God's sake."

I slammed my art journal shut, hiding the drawing I'd just made called "Momclops."

"I've got a plane to catch and Grandma needs you," Mom said, pressing the wheeliebag handle into my hand and latching onto her own perfectly matched luggage set.

"I still don't get why Grams has to move. She's happy there on the farm."

"Sylvie, she's not right. You know that. Ever since Grandpa Chuck died, she's been forgetting things. Important things. It's not safe for her to live alone anymore."

Mom clicked open the Lexus trunk. "I can stay with her," I said, dumping my backpack into the trunk. "You're gone all the time anyway."

Mom gave me The Look—one eye wide under an arched brow, the other so narrow it practically disappeared. "You're going to college, kiddo. Not babysitting your grandmother."

I felt my eyes bug. Grams would be so pissed if she heard that. "Babysitting." She was content on the farm with her horses and cat. Besides, Aunt Kate was right next door.

"But really, why the big rush?"

"Because I need you to pack up and clear out the house. I know you've loved going there every summer, but things change. It's time to grow up and let the farm go."

Car doors slammed. My imagination hid from the eye in the middle of Mom's forehead. It was always better to let her think she was in control of the universe.

"Here's my travel schedule," Mom handed me a list of all the stops she was scheduled to make presenting the latest hot new drug. "I'm starting in Zurich. And I need you to get Grams to her appointment at the retirement home as we planned."

"As *you* planned," I said before I could stop myself.

Mom gave me The Look again and then pretty much ignored me once we hit I-5.

My stomach started to ache. I wanted this summer to be like the sixteen summers we'd had before. Just riding, messing with the horses, adventuring with Pen. Instead, I felt like a double agent sent to hijack Grams.

Des Moines, Auburn, the Tacoma Dome blurred by.

"I can't believe I'm going to miss your birthday this year," Mom broke our silence as we crossed the Narrows Bridge. The guilt must have gotten to her.

"You always do." I looked down at the rough water far below.

"Oh, not true!" she wailed. "I always call."

I gave her a lame-ass smile.

"Sylvie, you know I do all this for you." Mom's voice went pissy.

"Private school, college, none of it's free."

I attempted to look appreciative even though I'd heard this speech like four hundred times. "It's good we're here for Grams," I said, using "we" even though it felt like it was really just me.

"Exactly," Mom said, turning the car into Grams's driveway.

When we pulled up, Grams emerged from the canopy of vine maples near the front door of the big house. I jumped out of the car and met her on the walk.

"Sylvie, honey." She spread her arms and wrapped me in a big hug. "I'm so glad you're here."

"I'm here too," said Mom, hurrying to give Grams a stiff hug.

"Are you going somewhere?" Grams looked at Mom, eyes questioning. "You're always running away."

"Don't be silly," said Mom. "I told you I was going to Zurich to help launch a new fertility drug. I'm not running away. I'll be back before you know I left." Mom blew a kiss as she hurried back to the car. "Love you! I'll call you."

Grams and I waved back. "See you in August," I said.

"Be good," said Grams beneath the rumble of the car engine.

"So we can be bad," I said, reaching for Grams's hand. She laughed and swatted my butt. "What's all this about you moving?" I asked.

"Oh dear," Grams touched my arm. "I don't know. Nobody ever tells me anything. But your mother and aunt Kate seem to be hell bent on getting rid of all my things. I don't like it one bit."

I found out what she meant the next day when Aunt Kate came over demanding I help clean the barn. She sent me up into the hayloft while she shouted orders from below. Once I was up there, though, I could see why Aunt Kate wanted to haul everything to the burn pile before it spontaneously combusted and burned the barn.

"Just shove it!" yelled Aunt Kate as she maneuvered the garden cart beneath the hayloft door like a firefighter positioning an air bag.

"This thing is nasty." I stood in the hayloft of the horse barn, alfalfa and cobwebs clinging to the sleeve of my ratty sweatshirt. Jeans coated with hay dust, I was glad I'd chosen tall barn boots instead of sneakers. Who knew what lurked amidst the piles of crap Grandpa Chuck had heaped up there over the years?

"Don't be such a wuss, Sylvie. Just shove the box out the door!"

Aunt Kate stared up at me with her hands on her hips and the belly of her overalls bulging with twins. Six-plus months along. Gramps woulda been proud.

I bit my lip and tried to shake off the image from last fall of Grandpa Chuck in his coffin lying still and cold as old meatloaf. It wasn't the memory I was after, so I slapped my leather gloves together and leaned out the door. "We're burning it *all*, right?"

"Right. We're finally finishing what Dad started years ago." Kate pushed her wire-rimmed glasses up on her nose. Her long, straight hair had been pulled back in a French braid, super tame compared to my wild, bronzy curls. "Get a move on, we've gotta get back to the burn pile."

I thought of Mom on tour in Zurich and the fleeting dream I'd had that she'd let me go along to celebrate my seventeenth birthday. But she needed me here. No way would she be stuck amidst the creepers.

Pulling my bandana up over my nose and mouth, cowboy style, I heaved against the moldy, hay-strewn box. It barely slid an inch. I growled and shoved at the box again. It burped dust and junk mail. Something rustled. Good thing Mom wasn't here; she'd be freaking out about dust mites and rabid rodents. Pen, on the other hand, would probably search the box for a new pet.

Me? I just wanted to get it done. So I lifted the front edge of the box over the metal lip that edged the doorway and shoved the ancient container of decaying bank statements and rancid receipts out the hayloft door. "Banzai!" I yelled.

In a weird, slow-motion moment, the box floated toward the cart, landing hard and exploding into a mini-mushroom cloud. Dust billowed. Tiny white moths flittered blindly from the box's jumbled depths.

Next, I grabbed a bundle of old-timey costumes Grandpa Chuck had bought during a bout of Auction Fever. Speckled with moth casings and crusted with mouse pee and dried blood from barn-cat birthings, I held my breath as they sailed toward the cart.

"That's good!" yelled Kate. "Now get down here and help me push."

I scrambled down the loft ladder and heaved against the metal handle of the wooden cart. "Shove this, push that. Geez, you're almost as bad as my mom," I said as we pushed the cart through the gate into the hillside pasture.

"Impossible," said Kate. "She'd have hired all this out."

"She did." I smiled. "Only she went with the Economy Plan—me."

Kate bumped my shoulder. "Well, I for one am glad she did."

For that moment, I was glad to be there too. I thought back to my first summers with Grams and Grandpa Chuck—when the big, shingled house had been brand new and the pasture grass was taller than me. Over the years, hungry horses and eroding rains had transformed the hillside pasture into a sparse collection of stubborn nubs. It was still home, though, complete with the crooked shingle line on the barn where Gramps had let me nail on new siding when I was five. Later on, we'd built a troll bridge across the creek in the horse pasture that became a cross-country jump as I grew older and braver. Even the bulbs and primroses Grams and I planted under the trees along the driveway still bloomed every year.

Above it all, stood the big house; three stories high, with a balcony off the living room where you could stand on your tiptoes and see Crescent Harbor filled with fishing boats. Below the balcony was the lower floor with Grams's big kitchen and Grandpa Chuck's patio with its black-shrouded gas barbeque. He used to cook salmon and singe hot dogs there nearly every Sunday night. I hated salmon, but loved the ritual.

As Kate and I pushed the wooden cart over the bumpy pasture, a daddy longlegs emerged from the pile of paper rubble. He paused, teetering on web-thin legs like a junkman surveying his yard. As if on his command, the breeze shot scents of mildew and mouse shit up our noses.

"Ugh! I can barely breathe," Kate said, pulling the neck of her T-shirt over her nose.

"Don't be such a wuss." I said from behind my bandana.

She sneered at me, a look she'd no doubt perfected on Mom when they were kids. With a spread of seven years between them, it was no big surprise that they were as different as OshKosh and Oscar de la Renta.

Once we'd rolled the cart up to the fire, Kate and I hurled handfuls of old hay onto the embers. Flames leapt, so the grungy costumes went next, the fire gulping them like a starving serpent. Next we tossed rain-warped junk mail and crumpled checks into the spiraling flames and watched them curl into flakes of black ash.

"Why don't we just torch the whole thing?" I said, grabbing a huge handful of junk mail and bank statements and piling it onto the fire.

"Can't do that," said Kate, contorting her bushy eyebrows. "You'll smother the flames."

"Whatever." I was already 100 percent sick of always being told what to do. Even though the flames spluttered as Kate predicted, I tossed more mold-splotched files onto the fire anyway.

"Sylvie, stop!" Kate commanded.

I stepped back from the fire as Scout, our 27-year-old Morgan gelding, plodded up behind me to lip alfalfa bits out of my hair. "Hey buddy." I scratched his neck and let Kate handle feeding the fire. Scout pushed closer, searching my pockets for treats. He'd grown thin since last summer and his tail was crusted with poop. "Sorry dude, no carrot mush or applesauce in there." Scout nudged me with his nose. I laughed and went back to feeding Grandpa Chuck's crapola to the flames.

Scout's shoes clicked on loose pasture stones as he wandered over to try Kate. "It's hell getting old, isn't it?" she said, scratching the base of his ear.

Not to be left out, Kate's ancient Thoroughbred, Gulliver, crowded in for attention. Neither of the two arthritic horses could be ridden much anymore, but they'd become part of the family so Grams kept on eking out money for feed. Mom never got the horse thing, but for me and Kate and Grams, they were part of us. Grams still had all of our horse show ribbons hanging in the mud hall.

With Kate and the horses tangled in a love fest, I turned back to the boxes. Tossing an empty shoebox into the fire, I realized that the one big box I'd shoved out the hayloft door was actually three boxes of stuff mashed into one. Grandpa Chuck had been the master of the "dump box"—the move where he swept everything from the top of his desk into a giant box to make room for a party bar. But this was different.

Curious, I lifted one flap of the inner box to check for critters, finding a sea of curled black-and-white photographs instead. Unknown faces stared up at me as if drowning in time, and floating on the surface was a small red book. I opened the other flaps to investigate. Smaller than my art journal, the red book's edges were tattered and the spine was cracked. The year 1945 was stamped in white on its front cover. When I picked it up, it smelled of musty boy sweat and gunpowder. Maybe I'd been inhaling too much smoke, but the writing on the page seemed to float.

Stand down on mission—Mussolini was hung and shot today or yesterday in Milano. Good deal. The war is going pretty well. Went down to the shack and did some printing. No mail.

"Hey Kate," I said, not taking my eyes off the page.
"Hey what?"
"I think I found Grandpa Chuck's World War II diary."

CHAPTER TWO

ENGAGEMENT PHOTOS

Honey-colored light seeped through a crack in the heavy gray clouds overhead. "No way," Kate said. She stepped toward me and reached for the book.

I turned to keep her from taking it. "Way," I said, way more intrigued with this than my own plain, black art journal filled with notes and ridiculous Momclops poems.

"He never wanted to talk about the war," she said, leaning over my shoulder as I let the pages flip open in my hands.

30 MARZO–March; LUNEDI–Monday

Went out to the line to get some pictures on preflighting, etc. New crew chief on the ship, Cooper—good man. One letter from Merrilee, one from Mother. News from Smitty—doing fine.

A breeze rolled up the pasture. I wanted to keep the red book forever. It reminded me of the note I stole off Grandpa Chuck's mirror. The one in fountain pen handwriting that said "I am the master of my fate; I am the captain of my soul."

"Where'd you find this?" Kate asked, grabbing the book and tucking it under her arm.

I nodded at the water-stained, sagging box filled with curled photographs and mouse-chewed letters.

Kate knelt down to dig through the box. Dust spiraled upward like spirits of the dead.

"Gimme that journal," I said.

Instead, Kate held up a handful of photos. "Check these out," she said. The first photograph showed six guys posed in front of a plane. The other was a painting of a woman, wearing nothing but an operator's headset and a little bitty skirt.

I snorted. "That chick belongs in the Hooters Hall of Fame."

Kate laughed and blew dust off another photo. "Hey, here's Dad." She held up a headshot of a young guy who looked totally unfamiliar except for his smile. It was the same as Kate's—wide, with a slight gap between the front teeth. The guy was dressed in a slick-pressed shirt, a uniform hat, and aviator sunglasses.

"That's Grandpa Chuck? He was decently cute," I said. "No wonder Grams fell for him."

Kate dug deeper into the box and picked up a letter. The paper was brittle and mice had munched one of the folds, leaving a hole in the middle. I slid the diary from under her arm as she began to read out loud.

> *My Dear Little Soldier Boy,*
>
> *I shudder when I think of you being in the Air Corps. Do you remember when you were about seven, you were at the house one day, and I let you run the Hoover sweeper? You were thrilled to death because it sounded like an airplane. I wonder if that terrible roaring of motors will always thrill you....*

It was weird, that feeling of spying on someone's secret life. But I couldn't resist reaching into the time-warped photos like I was fishing for a winning raffle ticket. When I pulled out my prize, though, I just about dropped it. "Wait a sec," I said, flashing the snapshot at Kate. "Who's this guy kissing Grams?"

Kate leaned in to study the black-and-white print. For a second, her eyes went squinty, brows furled. Then nothing—her face blank. "I don't know," she said. "But it sure isn't Dad."

I wiped about a hundred years of dust from the back of the picture to uncover the words written there. "Our engagement in Denver. Love you always, Bish."

"Bish?" My throat tightened. "And here I thought Grams and Grandpa Chuck had been together since God made dirt."

Deep wrinkles appeared in Kate's forehead. She pulled another photo from the box. It was a young guy in a leather jacket with goggles pushed up on his forehead, poking his head out an airplane window. Written along the bottom edge of the photo was "50th Mission, April 1945."

It was Grams's lover boy, again. Even though he stared into the distance, I would have sworn his eyes followed mine. It made me flush, like the fire had shot up about 5,000 degrees even though there was barely a flame. "Do you know that guy?" I asked.

Kate didn't answer so I slid the mission picture from between her fingers. I studied the handwriting, the guy's leather jacket, his goggles, the ring on his right hand. Something about it made me shiver and drop the picture. Kate looked up, but before she could quiz me, the sliding glass door at the big house rumbled.

Scout's ears pricked and he limped over to meet Grams and Dixon, Kate's three-year-old, at the pasture fence. "Hey girls, how's it going?" Grams called. "Throwing out more of my treasures?" Her voice was a combination of resentment and gratitude.

"Old crap, Mom," said Kate. "Not treasures."

"Except this stuff," I said, holding up the diary and engagement photo. I reached for the mission picture as a breeze spun it toward the fire. I raced after it, but the flames won. Frustrated and still curious, I turned to Grams. "So who's Bish?" I yelled across the pasture.

Kate put her hand on my arm. "Don't," she whispered. "Not now."

I shrugged out of Kate's grip and met Grams at the pasture gate. She squinted at the engagement picture, then took it eagerly into her hands. For a second, her face lit up, then her shoulders drooped and she walked past me, zombie-like, toward the fire. "He was just a boy I knew a long time ago."

Grams stared deep into the flames. Dixon ran to Kate and she lifted him to the safety of her hip.

"But you were engaged to him. Right?" Something deep inside me needed to know. "Why didn't you just marry him?"

Grams's jaw tightened. "He wanted to fly. Bomber boys had to be single."

"But you were engaged."

Grams nodded, her eyes distant.

"How'd you meet? How old were you?" I kept pushing, even though I knew from her body language I shouldn't.

"We went to the same high school," she said, as if reading the past in the flames of the fire. "Dad wasn't too thrilled about my seeing an older boy—but we had such fun." Grams pressed the engagement photo to her heart.

"Do you think Grandpa Chuck really meant to burn all this stuff?" I asked.

Grams sighed. "Sylvie, honey, Chuck never meant to burn all this. I did." She let the picture slide from her fingers into the flames. "Just never got around to it." She watched the photo contort and darken into ash. I ached to grab it from the fire and demand the whole story. But it was too late—the photo was gone and Grams's face had changed from sad to mad.

"Oh, hell," she said, dropping the diary into the ash at the edge of the fire. "Just burn it all." Grams headed back to the house, gathering the fronts of Grandpa Chuck's old shirt around her. Kate hurried after her, wrapping Grams in a sideways hug. Even Dixon patted Grams's shoulder as if he too felt her pain.

I wanted to run after them—shout that I was sorry—be the one to comfort Grams. I never meant to make her mad, or sad, or whatever she was right then. But I was torn between leaving things be and digging out the truth. Part of me wanted to know—needed to know. Part of me was pissed at them for keeping secrets.

Shifting smoke snapped me into action. I kicked the singed diary out of the fire, and went back to the box of old photos. My fingers pulled a picture out of the pile. My mind hoped for Grandpa Chuck. "I wish you were here," I whispered, thinking of his big dopey smile. But the picture wasn't Grandpa Chuck, it was Grams's guy again. Same leather jacket, khakis, goggles swapped for a funky baseball cap. He was smiling and looking cool. I sneered at the photo. "Who the hell are you?" I hissed.

"Look in the diary." The voice was in my head, but it wasn't mine.

Hands trembling, I picked up the red diary and opened it to the front page.

"The Private Diary of Keith D. Bishop" was written there. The name "Bish" was scrawled below that. The handwriting looked familiar, although it finally occurred to me that it wasn't Grandpa Chuck's. There was a distinct shape to the K, as if it was the beginning of a star. The rest was a mix of caps and small letters. I'd seen it somewhere...somewhere...like on the note I'd swiped from Grandpa Chuck's bathroom mirror.

Grandpa Chuck had a collection of what he called his "power of positive thinking notes," and he'd read them everyday. They were still there, taped to the bathroom mirror—except the torn and yellowed one I'd stolen last summer and pasted into my art journal.

I am the master of my fate; I am the captain of my soul.

I'd always wondered what it meant. Sweat trickled down the side of my face. The handwriting on the note and in the diary were totally the same. "Who are you?" I demanded, staring at the picture.

A gust of wind rolled up the pasture. "What do you mean, 'Who am I?' Who are you?"

My head snapped up. Eyes blinked. There, in the smoke of the fire was the guy from the 50th mission picture. He frowned and stepped out of the flames.

I practically rolled over backwards into the dirt and dead grass of the pasture.

"It's about damn time," he said. "And how."

"What are you talking about?" I asked. Somehow my feet pushed against my legs, and my legs pushed against my torso till I was standing nearly eye-to-eye with him. No way was he much older than me. "Time for what?"

He pulled a little card out of his pocket, glanced at it and put it back. "I'm looking for one Sylvie B. Stevens. You know her?"

"Maybe," I said, shoving my shaking hands into the back pockets of my jeans. "What do you want with her?"

He looked each way as if checking for spies and took a step closer. "Here's the deal. I've got a 21-day furlough to complete a Final Mission and she's my conduit." He glanced at his watch. "I've got exactly 504 hours to get to Ala and deliver a message. Sylvie's my go-to. Can't do it without her, in fact. If you know her, I need to get to her, and how."

CHAPTER THREE

LETTER FROM HOUND DOG

Surely I had been sniffing too much of something. I glanced at the house, then back to the fire, blinking my eyes and shaking my head; the guy had to be a hallucination. But he was still there. "Shit. You're Bish." The words sounded like air hissing from a tire.

"Who else would I be?" He dug his hands into his pockets and looked around, taking in the pasture, the big house, and the view to the harbor. "What year is it? Whose house is this?"

"You're kidding, right?" I toed the red diary that had once again fallen a little too close to the fire. "I thought ghosts knew everything."

"Oh, hell no. My buddies and I've been killing time playing Black Jack waiting for the go-ahead," he said with a snort. "Time's irrelevant when you're on stand-down. So no joke, what year is it?"

"It's 2003," I said. "And your fiancé, remember Merrilee, the girl you dumped in the war? This is her house."

"Holy mackerel." He whistled. "Sixty damn years. And I didn't dump her, missy." Bish squatted by the box of photos and tried to pick one up, but his fingers went right through. "I died, dammit. Death has a nasty way of ending an engagement."

"I guess," I fumbled for words while trying to shake off the heebie-jeebies. Chills skittered down my spine. I wanted to run, but I felt sort of sorry for him. I pulled an engagement photo from the box and held it up for him to see. He reached out again, his fingers lingering and semitransparent. "Must have been a big day," I said, but before the words were out, I was kissing young Grams, feeling the wetness of her lips, the soft wool of her coat beneath my hands, smelling her perfume, and hearing her giggle.

Both Bish and I dropped the picture. "What the hell?" I hissed, jerking away as the picture fluttered back into the box.

"So you are Sylvie B. Stevens," said Bish, smiling. "Only conduits can tap memories."

"Eeuuw. Says who?" I squirmed and walked a few steps away.

"Headquarters. Mission briefing. Just trust me on this. It could work to our favor."

"How so?" I was intrigued, but no way did I want him to know. I crossed my arms and tried to look bored.

Keith D. Bishop frowned at me. Frustration showed in the squint of his super blue eyes. "As in transferring a lot of essential info PDQ."

I snorted. "Yeah right, but keep that private stuff to yourself," I said. "I like my grandma, but no way do I want to make out with her."

Bish stood and shoved his hands back into his pockets. "So you're her granddaughter." A smirk flitted across his face. "That's just swell."

Rain spat at us. Gray clouds promised more.

"Best get my things out of the rain," said Bish. "They won't do a damn bit of good as paper pulp."

"Your things?" I said. "How so?"

"Stop asking questions and get moving." Bish glanced toward the big house as the glass door rumbled again. Scout nickered.

"Syee vee, Gamma says come get lunch." Dixon held up a triangle of bread.

"I'll be right there, Dix," I shouted back, hurrying to gather up all of Grams's—Bish's—whoever's—stuff into the one grunge-less box so I could carry it to cover. The workshop in the barn was safe enough. Grams hardly ever went in there—too many of Grandpa Chuck's tools. And even though this Bish dude had me so tweaked I wanted to puke, no way was I letting Grams burn all his stuff.

When I got to the workshop, there was an empty spot on the workbench, so I plopped the box there. Light streamed through the dirty window, and I eased away, afraid of what it might do to the contents of the box. There were hundreds of photos of guys and planes in there. Would they all come crawling out? My body twitched, my brain said "run" so I did, sprinting from the barn to the safety of the house and living, breathing people.

At lunch, I took one bite of egg salad sandwich but could barely swallow it. Dixon tried to get me to eat more, feeding me a potato chip and baby carrot, just like I'd often fed him. Back then, he was like a little cupid, yellow curly hair, dark eyes, perfect pink lips. When he wasn't throwing a temper tantrum, he was adorable.

Kate dozed in the cushy chair by the little woodstove, and Grams puttered in the kitchen. She put the teakettle in the refrigerator and wiped down the long counter. I gave half my sandwich to Dixon and took my plate to the sink.

"Sorry I made you mad out there, Grams," I said, wrapping my arms around her. "I didn't mean to."

"I know," she said, patting my arm. "I hate the idea of moving. So tired of it. Always stirs up too much dust from the past."

Dust and pain, I thought to myself. That's why Mom sent me to deal with it. I can't be hurt by what I don't know—or so she thinks. She's never been one to look back. And cleaning out Grams's house is all about that. Even with me, Mom shrugged off my love child status like a butterfly shedding a cocoon. "Keep your mind in the moment and your eye on the future," she often preached.

I rinsed my plate. "Do you know how lucky you are that you found the love of your life?" I said to Grams. "I'm still waiting for Mr. Right."

"You're young, dear." Grams patted my back.

"Same age as you were," I said, squeezing her arm. "Maybe older."

Grams put her finger over her lips to shush me. "Did I ever tell you that I took the train to Denver to see Bish? My sister went with me, but oooh, did we get in trouble with Daddy."

"And people call me a teenage deviant," I said, smiling. "That must have been when you two got engaged."

Grams squinched up her face like she was trying to remember something then gave up. "I don't know. It's been a long time."

I took her soft hand in mine and fingered the twining gold vines and deep-set diamond of her wedding ring. She still wore it despite Grandpa Chuck's death. "It's okay, Grams. I'll stop bugging you."

Grams kissed my cheek and crumpled into a chair at the table next to Dixon. He climbed into her lap, and Grams snuggled him in like she used to do with me. Opening the fridge door, I took out a water bottle and the teakettle, quietly placing the kettle back on the stove. Grams didn't need to be reminded of her mistakes. She was sad and frustrated enough.

"I'm heading back to the burn pile," I said, more curious than ever about Bish.

"Umm-hmmm," mumbled Kate, eyes still closed. Grams waved and nodded from her chair. Dixon had buried his face between Grams's neck and shoulder. I remembered the spot. It was good.

Of course, I didn't stay at the burn pile. Who could when a Star Trek tractor beam was pulling you to a stinky old box in the workshop? Besides, I was a sucker for mysteries.

"Yo, Bish," I said when I got back to the box. My voice seemed loud and echoey in the afternoon silence of the barn. "If you're here, stop messing with me."

There was no answer, no magical appearance. Maybe I was the one who was losing her mind, not Grams. I scanned the contents of the box. The corner of one letter poked above the pile. It caught my eye because the return address said "Bishop's Sports Shop, 104 Second Ave. SE, Puyallup, Washington." I slid it out of its envelope and unfolded the tan paper. Pencil-scrawled handwriting covered its pages.

May 14, 1943

Stow's Boarding House, Puyallup, Washington

Dear Bish,

I bet you are having a swell time. What I wouldn't give to travel cross-country like you. How did you like Chicago and all the big towns? What do you think of New York? You might have seen a good baseball game in New York, but Chicago isn't so hot. I hope you saw the Brooklyn Dodgers — they are the best.

Mother wrote to say she is proud to have three boys signed up for the service now. It was good you stopped in North Dakota to see her and the kids. How many of my friends did you see and what did they say? Did you see Bauer? He's the tall kid with the ass sticking out.

How about the family and all the little tots?

Everything is fine here. I haven't missed a minute of school since you left. I haven't spent much either, except for shoes and socks $9.60 (Regal). Also $15 dollars advance to Mrs. Stow. I hit Pick's Jackpot for $9 dollars and the next time I played I made $6 dollars clear. I don't think you would like it, but I thought I might as well hit it while it was hot. Don't get the idea that I'm a slot machine fiend because I can quit when I want to. I have saved about fifty dollars since you left. I don't figure that's bad at all.

It's five minutes to eleven now so I'll have to stop. The dinner bell is ringing. Have you been inducted into the Air Corps yet? Write soon, and make that letter thick!

Hound Dog (Warner E. Bishop)

P.S. Did you shoot that game of pool for me?

The last page was a letter from Bish back to Hound Dog.

July 19, 1943 — Miami Beach, Florida

Dear Hound Dog,

Sorry it's taken me so long to get this letter out. Seems I've been in constant motion ever since leaving town. You know how we whooped it up when I got word I'd made the grade for the Air Corps? It's been pretty much like that the whole way. I started Basic three days ago here in Miami Beach. Who would have thought they could take this place over like they have? The old resort hotels are barracks, the restaurants are mess halls, and the theaters are classrooms. The war is going full bore, and who knows for how long? I'm glad I got to see the family before coming here.

The folks are well enough. Ellendale, N.D., is another dusty town filled with churches and bars. Mother is set up there with all the little mites. Verla is her right-hand gal now that Dad and Eddy left for the shipyards in Bremerton. Guess all those years of blacksmithing will come in handy. You may have already heard, but we have a new little brother. Can't believe there are 15 of us Bishop kids now.

Chicago, New York, and Washington, D.C., were grand. Biggest damn cities I ever did see. All trains and taxis and people rushing by. Met another Air Corps fella from Washington headed to Basic on the train to Miami. Big, tall, quiet fella goes by Lefty. We're roommates now, along with another boy from Jersey (Smitty) and a Philly boy named Naussman. The officers say they gotta toughen us all up, see what we're made of, before they send us out to stomp the damn Japs and Nazis.

Speaking of basic, it's time to turn in. They make us jump outta bed in our skivvies at 5 a.m. on the nose. Keep up with school, and keep up with the saving. Don't lose it all in those damn slots.

Keep those letters coming,

Bish

P.S. Tell Merrilee she can write to me here at South Beach for the next five weeks. I'll send word to her through you like we planned. Tell her that before she knows it, I'll be flying my own plane.

17

What a life. He sounded totally pumped. No way would I be that positive if I'd just been drafted. I rifled through the box to find the crew shot Kate had held up briefly when we'd first found the box. Six guys posed in front of a plane with Bish kneeling in front.

"No way can you be real," I said.

The photo morphed as if I was wearing 3-D glasses. Light streamed through the workshop window again. I was back in the heat of the fire.

"Want to place a wager on that?" said Bish, startling me so bad I practically dumped over the box trying to steady myself. Photos, letters, and postcards spilled all over the place. Bish stood in the workshop doorway in full flight gear. Leather helmet and goggles, flight jacket, parachute, jumpsuit, and heavy brown leather boots. A yellow inflatable life vest was draped over his shoulders. "Reality is rarely what it seems—or what we wish for."

I scrambled to scoop up the scattered pictures and letters and toss them into the box. Part of me wanted them to be shut away and forgotten forever. The other part was burning to know more. The photo of Bish's crew balanced on Grandpa Chuck's big old hand drill and a rusty carriage wrench. I picked up the photo and held it up for Bish to see.

"Mission 17," said Bish. "Damn Mission 17. The one time our training crew flew in combat together. Ruined my life forever." He squinted hard and frowned. "We were supposed to be lucky. Lefty, Naussman, Feinstein, StuBoy, Valentine, and Bishop. We'd trained together in South Carolina and thought we were invincible." Bish clenched his teeth as if he were fighting back a wave of pain. "Boy, were we wrong."

There was a part of me that wanted to give the guy a hug. Clearly something had been messed up. But how do you hug a ghost? Instead, I took that moment to test a bizarre idea. Jabbing the photo into Bish's nebulous shape, I felt a familiar burn. Heat raced up my arm and I was sucked into chaos. The scream might have even been mine.

I'm in a plane, feet straining against a metal brace, hands on gun controls. Explosions everywhere. I stare straight down through a blister window at a stone building, a train, a truck. People strewn in the street. A woman, dead and bloody. A little girl kneels next to her. She lifts her face and stares at me, eyes full of fear. "Don't move," I pray. "Oh, God, don't move." My gloved hands are squeezing, shooting, unstoppable. Shells gather around my feet like a haul of fresh sardines. Sweat and gunpowder choke the air. The girl is running. "God dammit, no!" I yell.

In the next second, I was back in the workshop, heart pounding. "Damn fool girl." Bish scowled and turned away. "Don't you ever tap me without my go-ahead."

The little girl's eyes, full of fear and hate, flashed in my memory. The three bites of lunch surged in my gut. "Who was that?" I asked. "What was that?"

Bish rubbed a hand over his face. "Strafing run," he said, barely above a whisper.

"But that little girl? You shot her. I saw it."

"What the hell do you think this Final Mission is all about?" said Bish. "It ain't no milk run. I never wanted to be a kiddie killer."

Bish slumped onto an overturned crate with his head in his hands. His sadness seared through my body.

"No offense," I said. "But what am I supposed to do about it? You can't change the past."

Bish growled like a cornered animal. "The *signadora* said I could set things right if I delivered the *lamella*."

I had no friggin' clue what he was talking about, but it didn't seem like the time to push. Bish swept his helmet off and tugged at his hair. "But I lost it, and everything went to hell. My guts get blown out and instead of me, all my girl gets is a box of pictures, a sweat-stained jacket, and a diary I had no heart to finish."

"Which she kept all this time," I said. My hand shook as I set the picture back in the box. No way did I ever want to touch him or it again.

"What happened to her?" asked Bish. "A swell girl like her must have found somebody else—obviously raised a family."

I nodded. "She met my Grandpa Chuck. Up till a few months ago, they had 42 years, two kids, and two grandkids. Two more on the way."

Bish raised his eyebrows, but his whole body seemed deflated. "Holy mackerel. I'm glad for her, but that should have been me. I'd even put money on her wedding ring."

CHAPTER FOUR

PENELOPE

As Bish faded into the shifting sunlight, a million questions flooded my head. I needed Pen. Penelope Jones—summer riding buddy, awesomely exuberant friend, and card-carrying member of the Paranormal Detective Club.

I scrolled through the contacts on my phone and pressed Send.

The reply was so loud that even the dead could have heard it. "Hey girl. What's up?"

"I need your vast expertise with something."

"Sweet. Please tell me it's about my favorite subject," said Pen. "Guys. And by the way, we're still on for Alaska, right? I just got our ferry tickets."

"Alaska, totally. And guys, of course it is," I said, lying only a little. Never mind that they were dead guys.

"Then I'm on my way. In fact, I'm pulling into your driveway this very second."

I raced to the house to meet Pen at the front door. We stood face-to-face, still talking on our cell phones. My eyes bugged at her wild pants. "Oh, baby, I so need a paranormal detective right about now."

"Sorry. Membership expired," said Pen. "You do know that I only joined because I had the hots for that whacko ghost-hunter guy."

"But you know stuff about ghosts, right?" I motioned her toward the pasture as we snapped our phones shut.

"Way more than I ever wanted," she said. "Why?"

"Well, speaking of whacko," I said, pausing. "You can add me to your list."

"Huh?" Pen sniffed at my dusty, smoky clothes. I eyed Pen's crazy-ass pants. They were a wild blend of green, purple, and orange in bold geometric shapes that made her look like a walking piece of movie theater carpet.

She noticed that I noticed. "How about these?" She swaggled her hips. "Value Village special."

"I can see why," I said, smiling. She smacked me on the arm and we both cracked up. Pen and I had been riding pals practically since our first horse show. Even though she was raised Catholic, she was into crystals, psychics, and all kinds of weird shit. She had big boobs and a big laugh and a bigger heart that got her into—and out of—all sorts of trouble. She slid her phone into a back pocket and attempted to capture her long brown hair with a scrunchie. Bright orange peace signs dangled from her ears.

"So what's the big paranormal emergency?" She threw her arm around me. I put my finger over my lips and slipped through the gap in the fence to head to the burn pile. The fire still smoked despite the rain, so I raked the embers apart to stop the burn. I was only killing time.

"Spit it out, Syl. Why are we standing in the rain?"

Talking to Penelope Jones was like gulping Truth Serum. "Because I-I think I saw a ghost."

Pen shrieked. "Oh, my God, where?"

"Right here," I said. "In the smoke. He stepped out of the fire. Then again down in the workshop."

"No shit," she said. "I went to three of those PDC meetings and not one of them had actually seen a ghost. This is so cool."

"Seriously, I need your help. I'm afraid I'm going crazy." I started to tell her the whole story, but Grams called to me from the patio.

"Sylvie? I made a sandwich for you."

Grams had forgotten I'd already had one.

"Hi Mrs. S!" Pen waved to Grams. "It's been way too long."

Grams waved back. "Hey you," she said as Pen trotted over and wrapped Grams in a double-D hug. "Where have you been?"

"School," said Pen. "But now that Sylvie's here, watch out. I'll be bugging you all the time."

"Those are some pants," said Grams.

"One of a kind," said Pen. "Well, maybe."

"Just like you," Grams said, smiling. I could tell she was covering for not being able to remember Penelope's name. "Come in. Have a sandwich."

"We'll be there in a minute, Grams," I yelled, pointing at the fire. Grams waved and headed back into the house.

Pen stared at the house a while before walking back to me. "I think your Grandpa's spirit is still here, you know," she said.

"No shit, there's a spirit." I tossed the rake into the garden cart. "But it isn't Grandpa Chuck. It's some guy Grams was engaged to during the war."

"Woohoo. Go, Grams." Pen smiled her bad-girl smile. "So you've actually seen him? Is he cute?"

I shrugged and twisted my mouth. My insides were twisting too. "Talked to him even."

Pen looked at me like I was a bug on a pin in a science display. "Wow. You always were way more tuned in than me. I try so hard, but I get nothing. You don't give a rip and you get a real live spirit."

"Technically, dead," I said.

Pen blew me off with a roll of her eyes and a little psh sound. "What did he want? Spirits hardly ever show up without a reason."

"Something about a final mission. Said he needs my help."

Pen's perfectly shaped brows went wild, a sign she'd discovered deep thought. "Help with what?"

I shrugged. "He wants me to deliver some message." I kicked at a dying ember. "Only I get the sense there's a lot more to it than that."

"Did you tell him you'd do it?"

"No," I said. "He freaked me out. Said I'm his conduit." I bit my lower lip and tried to erase the memory of French-kissing my grandma, of that little girl's eyes.

Pen paced back and forth. "Those paranormal detective wannabes would be peeing themselves right about now. Apparently it's extremely ultimately awesomely cool to be a conduit—they're practically legendary. But I go more by what the psychic-types say. As in if you go by the old ways, you two were linked by the Fates when he was still alive. You're his only way into this dimension. This shit doesn't happen by accident. Lots of things have to line up in order for it to work."

I picked alfalfa off my sleeve. "Such as?"

Pen shrugged. "I missed that meeting because Whacko Guy and I broke up. But I'm guessing you did something that opened the passageway."

"I didn't do anything," I said. "I just wanted to know who the guy in the picture was because Aunt Kate and Grams were acting so weird. Next thing I know, there he is telling me 'we' have less than 21 days."

Pen pressed her lips together in a rumpled frown. "For?"

"Completing his mission."

Pen grabbed the hose we kept fireside and started spraying the ash and embers. Steam hissed and swirled skyward. "And if I know you like you know I know you," she said finally. "You're gonna do it." Pen switched off the hose and walked it back to the water trough by the fence.

I thought of Bish nearly in tears in the workshop, of the little girl, of Grams's failing memory. Lifting the handle of the empty cart, I met Pen as we walked down the hill to the barn. "Of course I am. I just have no idea how."

CHAPTER FIVE

StuBoy & Valentine

"So, who is this Bish guy, really?" Pen asked once we had transferred Bish's stash to a new file box and hauled it up to my room, out of Grams's line of sight.

"I'm not totally sure," I said. "All I know is that he died in World War II when he and Grams were engaged." Pen picked through the box while I changed out of dirty, wet jeans into sweats.

"Grams was only about 16 when they started dating."

"So why not just ask your Grams?" Pen pulled a picture out of the box and wiped the dust off on her pants.

"One minute she says she wants to burn everything," I explained. "The next she can't remember why. Then she's telling me about sneaking away to Denver on the train to see him." I jerked at the drawstring on my sweats. "It's totally random."

"Mmm, yummy," said Pen, not even paying attention to me. "Who's this?"

She held up the same picture of young Grandpa Chuck in his aviator glasses that Kate had pulled out earlier. "He's pretty fine. I could use a World War II boyfriend."

"Eeuuw, that's my Grandpa Chuck."

"Seriously?" said Pen, playing at being offended. "Then why does it say 'Always, Smitty'?"

I grabbed the photo and looked at it under my desk light. Sure enough, "Smitty" was signed at the bottom. Now, the person I really needed to talk to was Bish.

I set the photo on the desk and reached in to wriggle a smallish box with gray metal edging from the tangle of curled photos. It was smooth-pressed tan cardboard, and the torn label on its top said, "-chester Optical – Aviation Kit." My breath caught as I slid off the lid. What if there was some dead little critter inside? Instead, there was a slightly crusty pair of goggles nested among random bits of paper. Pen plucked a pink square from the mix—a ticket to the Museo

Vaticano in Rome. Next we found a scrunched-up ticket to Pompeii, a pamphlet of brittle paper pages called "A Soldier's Guide to Rome," and a red, white, and blue English-Italian phrase book held together with rusting staples.

"Siete voi il signor X?" I said to Pen.

She looked over my shoulder as I flipped through the phrase book. *"Possiamo avere in interpetre?"* she responded.

"Oh, baby, we totally need an interpreter for all this stuff," I said. *"Rispondete alle mie domande.* Hear that Bish? Answer my questions."

The goggle box began to seem like Mary Poppins's bottomless bag, because even after all that, we managed to score an enlisted man's pass from Greenville, South Carolina; instructions for using the goggles; and a set of mouse-chewed postcards from a gunnery school in Florida.

The art and color of the postcards was like a blazing sunset in the midst of all the black-and-white photos and papers. "Greetings from Flexible Gunnery School Ft. Myers, Fla." was printed above a wide palm-lined roadway. Airplanes flew in formation above it all. As I flipped the musty cards open to a mix of gunner training and beautiful-Florida scenes, Pen went on a manhunt. She plucked a picture out of the box. "He's too serious," she said, studying another dusty print of Bish's 50th Mission photo.

"But that's the guy—Bish," I said.

"He looks totally bummed out," said Pen. "I need someone fun."

"They were at war, Pen." I scanned the room, sensing Bish, but not seeing him. "Maybe he was tired of being shot at."

A breeze ruffled the curtain and flicked over a couple of photos on the desk. "This one looks like a rat-bastard," said Pen. I glanced over to see a squinty-eyed guy with the name TETRO on his uniform coat. Pen dropped the picture and picked up another. "How about this one? Oh yeah, this guy might do," she said, holding up the small, squarish picture.

I had to agree, the new guy was super cute. He had a sweet boy-next-door smile, despite a stained sweatshirt and flipped up baseball cap.

Pen smiled. "He looks like fun. I'll take him."

"What for?"

"Duh. My World War II boyfriend." Pen said it as if it wasn't weird and twisted at all. But then, over the years I'd known her she'd had a truckload of boyfriends—some real, some imaginary. There were construction boyfriends—guys working on nearby construction crews that the girls watched but never spoke to. There was Biker Boy, Granola Guy, and Magazine Man. The first two were real; the last, in a picture stuck to her bedroom wall. Pen even had an Olympic boyfriend—the one who made watching day after day of track events tolerable. Why shouldn't she have a World War II boyfriend? I doubt Bagger Boy at the grocery store would mind.

"Okay, take it," I said.

"Oh, no, no," said Pen, handing me the photo. "I don't want the picture. I want you to call him out. You should find yourself a World War II boyfriend too." She handed me two other photos. One was a Poindexter-ish dude, standing too tall and stiff in a uniform. The other was a more sultry hunk type wearing a white t-shirt and khakis, perched sideways on a windowsill. Much more my type. I was tempted, but I snapped out of it.

"Oh, no, no, no," I said, handing the pictures back. "That's too weird. And besides, why would you want a boyfriend you can't see or hear?"

"Might be the best kind. Just try." Pen gave me her most pathetic look, all melty and sad eyed. "If you called out that Bish guy, you can do it for them. Just say some magic words or something." She shoved the pictures in my face again. I rolled my eyes.

"Pleeeeeezze," said Pen. "He might be able to give you more info."

I was tempted. Answers would be good.

Pen smiled. "I can tell you want to...."

In that moment, I was a combo pack of freaked out and totally intrigued. But I honestly had no clue what to do. Then I figured I'd just fake it to shut her up.

"Okay," I said, clearing a space on the desk. "Put it there." Pen placed the picture of Happy Guy on the desk. I spread my hands above the photo and did my best to make up some crazy shit. "Ooglie booglie boo," I said, eyes closed, fingers wiggling. "I am calling you, to jump right out and give a shout. Ooglie booglie boo."

Pen made a hissing sound. "You're not taking this very seriously."

"Oh, come on, Pen," I said, opening my eyes to see that she had placed Windowsill Poser's picture next to Happy Guy. Shit. Thank God nothing happened. "You don't seriously think that ghosts can crawl out of photographs, do you?"

"Spirits," said Pen, hands on hips. "They're spirits, not just ghosts. And if what you said about Bish coming out of a picture in the fire is true, you have a gift. You're just too stubborn and stupid to see it."

"Scared, more like," I muttered.

Pen moved toward the door. "What's to be scared of? Don't you think that Bish guy is scared too? Imagine having your whole existence dependant on a stranger."

"He's not dependant on me. Anyone could do it." I bit at a nail, which I hardly ever do.

"Nope, not true," said Pen, shaking her head and crossing the hallway to the bathroom. "I'd bet real money that you're his only hope. Own it, girl, before I kick you in the head."

Pen slammed the bathroom door.

"She's right, you know."

I snapped around, expecting to find Bish, but instead I was face to face with Pen's smiling World War II boyfriend.

"You *are* Bish's only hope," he said. "He's been on standby a darn long time waitin' for you. And we're here to see you do right by him."

Windowsill Poser materialized across the room in front of my bedroom window looking even more ripped than he did in the murky little photo he came out of. He didn't say anything, just slid his hands in his pockets and pressed his lips together. A killer dimple appeared in one cheek.

"Then riddle me this, boys." I put my hands on my hips, determined to a) not show any fear, and b) blast them with my most urgent question. "Who is this Bish guy, really, and why do I have to be the one to help him?"

CHAPTER SIX

THE YEARBOOK

Before I got an answer, the doorbell rang and the ghost boys disappeared. Pen and I jogged down the stairs to find an old guy with a goatee, bow tie, and suspenders standing beyond the six-paned Dutch door.

"I've got it, Grams," I yelled. When I opened the door, Goatee Guy's beady eyes darted into every corner before settling on me. He cleared his throat.

"I'm Edwin Estby, from Books Etc." He said it like we were supposed to care. "Is Merrilee in? She called about selling some books."

I shrugged. Grams had been selling lots of stuff lately—Grandpa Chuck's gold cuff links and rings, the shiny red cart Scout once pulled. She acted like all these people were doing us a favor, but to me they were a bunch of scavengers, vultures circling above Grandpa Chuck's carcass.

"Not enough people wear suspenders these days," said Pen, throwing me for a loop. I bit my lip to keep myself from laughing. "They make a man look sooooo, how should I say...."

"Fruity Pants" came to mind, but Pen filled in with "distinguished."

"Why thank you, Miss—"

"Jones. Penelope Jones." She held out her hand for him to shake.

He did, limply, as Grams came up the steps from the kitchen, eyes rimmed red like she'd been crying. I wondered what was up, but it was so not the time to ask.

"Hi Edwin. It's good to see you," said Grams. She had a tissue in her hand, so she pointed instead of shook. "The books are up here." She led the way up the short set of stairs to Grandpa Chuck's big den. When she opened the door, Estby's eyes doubled with greed as he took in all the books and collectibles around the room. My eyes popped and my heart about stopped at the sight of Bish lounging in Grandpa Chuck's designer recliner. It was spooky how similar they were.

"Hey gal," Bish said. A smile the size of Kansas danced across his face. "Looks like your ooglie booglie bullpucky was good enough to get me a pair of guides."

My new buddies perched on top of the tall bookcase. They smiled and waved.

"Meet StuBoy Johnson, Engineer," said Bish as Pen's World War II Boyfriend raised a finger. "And Rodney Vals, Radio Operator."

Windowsill Poser did a smooth two-finger salute and smiled a smile that made my heart beat so hard it could have knocked the house down. "Valentine. Just call me Valentine."

"O-kay," I said, drawing out the syllables.

"What do you mean, 'Okay'?" whispered Pen. "Ol' Estby just offered your Grams a hundred bucks for all the books if we box them up and carry them to his car. That's a rip-off."

"She's right," said Bish. "Just my high school yearbook alone should be worth a hundred bucks."

He looked past me, his face going from smiley, to intense, to sad.

"Your yearbook is here?" I said, swiveling to see what had Bish going from flip to faraway.

"She's so old," Bish mumbled as he rose to his feet. My eyes dashed from Bish to Grams and back again.

Grams looked surprised at my surprise, but played along. "Of course, dear," she said, obviously clueless to the presence of Bish and the boys. "That old yearbook is here somewhere."

Bish was clearly stunned. Hadn't he expected to see her—guessed that she'd aged? Then I remembered that he didn't even know he'd landed in her backyard. You'd think their reconnaissance at "Headquarters" would be a little better than that. Even so, if you asked me, Grams still looked pretty dang cute.

"I collect old yearbooks," said Estby. He flipped through the books on the shelf like a fiend, but I found the yearbook first. It was old and tan-colored with "Vikings, 1941" on the cover.

"Wow," said Pen. "How cool is that?"

Bish snapped out of his oh-my-god-it's-Merrilee trance and shouted, "Don't sell it."

"Don't worry," I said.

Pen shook her head at my response, but crowded in with Grams to see as I flipped through the pages. "Smells like old gym locker," said Pen. She was right.

"Oh, goodness, there we are," said Grams. She ran her hand over the black-and-white picture. In it, she was a way young skinny bean in a dark dress and saddle shoes. Bish sported a business suit. "We met in debate class. He was a senior and I was a little freshman. He was much more outgoing than me—practically knew everybody in Puyallup. I couldn't believe he was interested in me."

"She had no idea what a gem she was," said Bish. "As fun and fresh as a new dollar bill. So unspoiled you wanted to save it forever."

"Those old yearbooks are the most marvelous bits of history," said Estby, inching closer to us.

"You've got that right," I said, snapping the annual closed. "But the self-help books, wow, those are gold." I nodded to the shelf full of them, and moved closer to Grams. "Grandma, can I talk to you for a sec?" I steered her to the living room. "Why are you selling the books? We haven't even had a chance to go through them yet. What if there's something we want to save?"

"Sylvie, honey, don't worry. None of these books are worth much. Besides, your mother says we need the money."

"But won't she and Kate flip out if they don't get to choose the books of Grandpa's they want?"

"There's not much I can do that will please your mother. Besides, if she really cared that much, she'd be here herself." That was Grams. So sweet and nice, but with x-ray vision that saw all the way to the soul.

My eyes wandered out over the pasture.

"Don't think I don't know you're feeling cooped up. I was young once too," Grams said. "I even ran off to visit a boy in Denver and South Carolina before he shipped out to the war. All the girls were doing it. But boy-oh-boy did it make my Dad mad."

My mind bounced between the Denver "kissing on the courthouse steps" engagement photo and Bish's 50th mission shot. Thankfully Grams had forgotten to be mad at me about Bish's box.

Pen poked her head around the corner. "Everything okay out here?"

Grams took my hand and pulled me back into the den. As I passed Pen, I handed her the yearbook. "Guard this with your life."

Estby had his glasses perched on his nose and a stack of books at his feet. He was still scanning the shelves.

Valentine saluted when we reappeared. "Don't worry, Sylvie-girl, we've been on watch," he said, his voice deep and droll.

"He only stuffed one book down his pants," said StuBoy, smiling.

Bish was perched on the ottoman of the designer recliner with his head in his hands. I looked at StuBoy and Valentine then jutted my chin at Bish.

"Poor fella just got a glimpse of Merrilee's wedding album," said StuBoy. "It about broke—"

"How about you boys go pour yourselves a nice cuppa shut-the-hell-up?" Bish snapped.

"Is that any way to talk to your pals?" said StuBoy.

I spotted the wedding album open on the shelf near Estby's cast-offs. Grams and young Grandpa Chuck were cutting a wedding cake. Of course it would tweak out Bish. Duh. I ached to ask StuBoy for the scoop, but with all the company I couldn't exactly go chatting with thin air.

Someone tapped my shoulder. "Earth to Sylvie," said Pen. "Your Grams wants us to get some boxes from the garage."

I blinked and pulled my head out of Bish's world. "I'm on it."

Pen followed me to the overstuffed garage and shut the door. "What gives?" she asked. "Was Bish there?"

"Oh yeah," I said, wondering if I should spill the beans about the guys.

"He saw Grams and Grandpa Chuck's wedding album and it got him all weirded out."

"Must be hard for him," said Pen.

"He's okay. He has help."

Pen squinched up her nose, clearly not getting it.

"StuBoy and Valentine," I said. "Your World War II Boyfriend and his buddy."

Pen shrieked so loud the entire garage echoed. "Oh, my God, do I look okay?"

I picked up a box and reached for the door handle. "They're ghosts, Pen. Seriously."

Back inside, the boys tagged along as Pen and I hauled boxes of books to Estby's car.

"Here, let me help with that," said Bish, reaching for the box.

"Thanks, but I thought you didn't do tangibles," I said.

Bish backed off. "Damn. I hate not being able to do anything."

Valentine slapped Bish's shoulder. "You can carry me."

Bish threw him a play punch. "I'll carry you, alright."

"Down boys," said StuBoy, pretending to twirl a lasso and rope them both. "Just hone your skills of psychokinesis and you can move all the boxes you like."

"Swell. Floating boxes," said Bish. "And that wouldn't be disturbing to Merrilee at all."

I snorted. Pen curled her lip at me. "You act like you're at some great party I can't go to."

I leaned into Pen as Grams and Estby swapped cash. "I'm sorry." StuBoy came over and gave Pen the puppy-eyes. "But if it makes you feel better, your World War II Boyfriend is cute. You were right."

Pen dropped her box of books into Estby's trunk, smiled, and closed her eyes. "Ah," she said, stretching her arms above her head. "I love the feeling of being right."

StuBoy jumped back, his eyeballs about popping out of their sockets. "Damn, she makes my calendar girl seem like an old maid."

Bish cleared his throat and walked part way up the circular driveway. He stopped and looked back at the big house. "At least Smitty set my girl up right," he said.

"What's that supposed to mean?" I asked.

Pen raised one eyebrow. "It means you've got the gift."

"It means the bastard stole my girl after I trusted him to deliver my gear," said Bish. "I needed her to remember me—to hold my jacket, wear my ring, know everything about where I'd been and what I'd done." He kicked at the gravel. "Damn chameleon stepped right in and took my life. My life. All because I never delivered that little *lamella*." Bish dug his hands into his pants pockets. "Never would have guessed a teenie piece of rolled up metal could have such power."

"A what?" I bit my lip, confused.

"The *lamella*," Bish said. "The tiny prayer note I need you to find and deliver to a church in Italy for the family of that little girl."

Pen looked sideways at me, lips curled. Bish's eyes swam with expectations.

"There's no way in hell I can get to Italy, let alone find some long lost bit of joint-sized metal."

"Italy?" said Pen. "I thought we were going to Alaska."

My clogs ground into the gravel as I turned back to the house. "We are."

CHAPTER SEVEN

POSTCARDS FROM FLORIDA

Of course there was no sleeping that night. The quiet was too loud. This mission-thing was too insane. Once Pen left to meet her real-life bagger-boy boyfriend and Bish and his buddies retreated to Headquarters or wherever they go when they were not bugging me, my mind ran over and over the impossibility of Bish's mission as Grams and I fed the horses and then fed ourselves.

Find a little prayer note and deliver it to Italy.

Bish made it sound so simple, but I knew better. I swallowed hard, my whole world spinning. I felt like Dorothy just after she'd been sucked up by a tornado and dropped into Oz.

Throwing back the covers, I peered out my window toward Kate's house, anxious to see familiar lights. I sighed, breathed, thought of the Jimmy Buffet song that always seemed to be playing over there. It had a line that went, "You only get two choices, havin' fun or freakin' out."

Since I preferred to leave the freaking-out part to others who do it better (insert Mom here), I decided to opt for fun. For me, fun equaled detective work. Fuck the flying monkeys. That's what Bish's big-ass guns were for.

The box was on my desk. The obsessive-compulsive side of my personality wanted to organize the jumble. The creative side wanted to make pictures and stories for each of the no-name guys. The frustrated side believed I'd find clues to the mysteries that were keeping me awake.

For instance, I understood how Bish could feel pissed at Grandpa Chuck for cashing in on the life he'd planned with Grams, but I didn't get how it all boiled down to this little *lamella*-thingy. Hell, I couldn't even figure out how Bish and Grandpa Chuck even knew each other that well in the first place.

Digging deep into the box, I set the letters in one pile, the postcards in another, and pictures of the few guys I recognized in still another. I unfolded a fragile piece of paper that said "Order for Transferred Man to Report for Induction." "Keith D. Bishop" was typed into the blank along with where he was supposed to report.

"Elk's Clubroom, 9 NE 3rd Ave. Miami, at 9am, on the 15th (Tues) day of June, 1943 to receive instructions relative to departure via Florida Motor Lines at 7:15am, on the 16th day of June, 1943."

"There has to be a reason." I found myself thinking out loud, trying to fit the pieces together. "What was he doing in Florida when he lived in Washington?"

"Simple. I was visiting my sister." Bish's voice came from beyond the desk light.

I about leapt into orbit. "Shit, don't scare me like that."

Bish moved into the light, hands in pockets. "Sorry. I thought you asked me a question."

"I thought you were off whooping it up with the boys."

"We don't get to do much whooping during a mission," said Bish. "Missions are all business. But when we get rest leave, stand back." He parked it on the spare bed.

"So where'd you really meet Grandpa Chuck—um, Smitty to you?"

"There," said Bish, nodding toward the induction notice. "Basic Training in Miami Beach. Those were some swell times."

I found the picture of young Grandpa Chuck in his swanky aviator glasses. "How come nobody else ever called him Smitty?" I asked.

Bish shrugged. "Lefty and I gave him that nickname when we heard his real name at roll call—Charles Smithson Stevens. Much too uppity. He was a Smitty back in those days, and how—some kinda smooth operator—but then we all were somebody different. Had to be, to survive." Bish rested his elbows on his knees.

"Is that where these postcards came from?" I held up the bright pack from the Ft. Myers Gunnery School.

Bish shook his head. "Gunnery school came later. After we'd been through Basic. Smitty left those for me when he disappeared on Classification Day."

"Disappeared?" He had me officially intrigued.

"I might be able to show you," Bish said, reaching for the bottom of the folding set I still had in my hand. "No guarantees."

When his fingers connected with the cards, the colors became brighter, and the air in the room hotter, more humid. Our eyes locked, and I gave a shaky nod. My stomach felt like I was buckling into a rollercoaster car at the front of the line.

Bish cleared his throat. "Smitty, Lefty, and I all showed up in Miami Beach that same day and wound up bunking together. We were mighty proud to have made it into the Air Corps and were cockier than roosters in a hen house. It was '43 and Roosevelt's men were recruiting replacement bomber crews. We were it. But I tell you, the early mornings nearly did us in."

I yawned, not because the story was boring, but because I honestly felt like I just rolled out of bed. Some guy in Army issue underwear was kicking another guy's bunk. "Lefty, you no-good SOB, get up!"

"Air raid drill!" I shouted. It took me a sec to realize the guy kicking the bunk was Smitty and that Bish's rollercoaster memory had taken off with me in the front car.

Sirens wail. Bells ring. There's no time to even think. Someone thumps on the door. "Out of the building! Line up for sound off!"

Lefty snoozes on, oblivious to the commotion. I look at Smitty and try to appear sad. "He had a hard night," I say.

"Ogling pretty young psychologists is hard work," Smitty says, smiling an impish smile. "With the help of all that bourbon, you'da thought he'd have lost his virginity at least."

I inch closer to Lefty's bunk. "Ain't that a shame?"

"Private Bishop, I do believe it's time for The Poet to awaken." Smitty points at the mattress corner and I nod. We each grab a corner and tip the sleeper out of bed.

"What the hell?" Lefty scrambles to his feet, nearly falls over.

Part of me wants to reach out and steady the poor guy, the other is locked into the confines of Bish's memory. "The Poet awakens!" I say as Smitty and I finally steady the tall, lanky, not-yet-a-man Private Leonard Allyn Poe. Each taking an arm, Smitty and I sling Lefty the Poet over our shoulders and haul him downstairs into the early morning air.

"Attennnnntiionnnnn!" The command shatters the darkness.

Boys line the streets of the tourist-town-turned-training-camp. Silhouettes of palm trees arch into the purple sky.

"Masochists," groans Lefty.

"Ever notice they only pull this crapola when they've

given us a night off the day before?" Smitty speaks to Lefty and me like a ventriloquist talking to his dummy.

"Shut it, Smitty," I whisper, steadying Lefty as he begins to wobble between us. We'd nicknamed him Lefty and The Poet, mostly because he was one and we liked the pun. Small pleasures.

"Did I actually recite Edward Lear to that girl last night?" Lefty asks.

"Oh yeah, you were the Limerick God," says Smitty. "That one about the girl from Berlin whose nose was as sharp as a pin really smoked that German gal."

"That bad, huh?" says The Poet.

Smitty nods. "Worse. Shakespeare woulda got ya a whole lot farther."

"Privates! Shut your pie holes! Did I say you could talk?" Sergeant Milhouse hammers the pavement, headed in our direction. "No! I did not say you could talk. You don't breathe unless I say so. Do you understand?" Milhouse glares. We shut it and stare straight ahead, darn sure his gaze can pierce metal, let alone human skin.

"Sound off!" bellows Milhouse.

We pipe our names into the salty morning air. All of us boys ache to do our bit for the country, and more than anything we want to fly. Everyone knows Basic is to weed out the weak and stupid. Not a one of us is either. "Bishop!" "Stevens!" we yell as names fly down the line like sparks along the wick of an explosive.

"Poe!"

"Frederick!"

"Williams!"

And on it goes, almost soothing, until the 50th name is uttered. Everyone is now wide-awake.

"Back to the barracks and be ready for mess at 0500 sharp! It's testing day, boys, and if I were you, I'd be searching the ground for four-leaf clovers."

"What's that supposed to mean?" I find myself saying the words even though I totally know. It's not as if I grew up under a log in South Dakota.

"Luck," says Lefty, in his quiet, droll way. "Apparently we're going to need it."

"Right," says Smitty. "Word on the street is that they

over recruited for pilots so they're diverting lots of fellas to bombardier, navigator, radio operator, engineers, and gunner training. And you know the saying." Smitty pauses for effect as the herd of men in underwear single-files past the mirrored walls of the lobby and up the stairs. "Go up a gunner, come down a goner."

I thought that was where Bish's memory ended, but he pushed on through the day, stopping at the moment he realized Smitty was missing. It was trippy being inside his mind like that—being him, on purpose. I coulda lived without the extra body parts, but whatever.

"Lefty, you seen Smitty?" I ask. "He was here a minute ago."

"One of the testing gals pulled him out of line when he went past," says Lefty.

"Lucky for him," I say, elbowing The Poet.

Lefty blushes. "I don't think it was because of his good looks."

"Well, we'll wrangle it outta him at mess."

But even after maze tracing and noonday mess, Smitty still hasn't shown up. He isn't in the dorm room when we return to rest and prep for PT. Even his bunk is wiped clean. Had Smitty cheated? Had he been kicked out?

"He can't have just disappeared," I say.

"We'll ask Milhouse, maybe he knows," Lefty says, scribbling in his not-so-blank book.

"Don't you even care? This isn't like Smitty," I say, scanning his top bunk for clues. "Where the hell did he go? He could have at least left word at the desk."

"We'll check for a message on the way to PT," Lefty mumbles.

I go to the window and look at the beach scene below. Ant-men are setting up some queer-looking obstacles for physical training. At least it might be something new. After eight weeks, the usual drills are plenty old. When will we actually learn something useful for combat? All the news reports try to soften the blow, but the Allies are taking a beating. And here, stuck in the sand, are thousands of guys ready and willing to jump in and do their part. Except, of course, those who disappeared. Where is Smitty, that SOB?

Lefty rips a page out of his book and hands it to me.

"A limerick?" I say. "Oh, that's swell. Our buddy goes missing and you write a confounded limerick?" My hand crumples the paper and throws it at Smitty's bed. "Jesus Christ."

"We'll find him," says Lefty. "Let's go ask around."

We become an interrogation squad, asking everyone we see if they'd seen Smitty. The only news we're able to gather is that Smitty was seen talking to some head-honcho colonel on the veranda of the officer's club. After that—poof. Nobody's seen him, and none of the higher ups are talking.

There isn't even any buzz at last mess. Everyone is too nervous about what comes next—the posting of technical school orders. I'd passed all my bombardier tests with flying colors. I'm sure I'll get that or radio operator all the way. Lefty, with his Jimmy Stewart looks and brilliant mind, is a shoe-in for pilot training.

By the time we make it to the hall, a swarm of boys buzzes around the classification boards. I find Lefty's name on the pilot training roster, right away. But as I run my finger down first the bombardier list then the radio operator list, there's not a Bishop or a Stevens to be found. I scan the pilot list just in case. No luck there, either.

"Sorry, Bish," says a guy from our barracks when he passes. "I know how bad you wanted pilot or bombardier."

What the hell is he talking about? As boys turn away from the lists puffed with pride or cloudy with disappointment, I keep on looking.

"You're here, Bish," says Lefty, quietly pointing to the Gunnery Training list.

"There must be some mistake," I say when I can finally focus on the name. BISHOP, Keith D. – Technical Gunnery School, Fort Lowry #2.

"The Army doesn't make mistakes," says Milhouse, pausing behind me.

"But Sir," I cut in. "I passed all the bombardier tests."

"Makes no matter," says Milhouse. "Headquarters says, 'Send us up some gunners,' we send them some gunners." Milhouse eases up a touch. "Truth of it is, we can train guys to fly planes and drop bombs, but we can't make 'em shrink to fit a tail blister or a turret ball. You gotta be small and feisty. That'd be you."

For the first time, Milhouse actually looks at Lefty and me as if we were human, not just lumps of clay to be shaped into fighting machines. "Sorry Bishop. They needed gunners, and it's our job to send them. If you really want to fly, that's your only option."

My stomach turns a loop-de-loop. "Go up a gunner, come down a goner," echoes in my brain. What about my Merrilee?

"Pack your gear boys," yells Milhouse above the din. "You're shipping out tomorrow at 1300 hours."

Until that moment, I'd never thought of myself as short or small. But as I hike up the stairs to our room, I begin to sort boys by height. Dammit. No matter how many smarts you have, height just isn't a thing you can change.

When we finally make it up the ten flights of stairs to our room, the piece of paper from Lefty's diary is on my bunk, still crinkled but smoothed out flat. I sprawl on the green, Army issue blanket and re-read the limerick.

> *Where's Smitty?*
> *There once was a man named Smit-Tee*
> *Who could hear a fish burp in the sea*
> *Until one strange day*
> *He was snatched right away*
> *By the nebulous net of the Arm-ee.*

"You know, Lefty, we're all little fish caught in the net of the Arm-ee," I say. "They just scoop us up and sort us out any old way they want to."

"You'll be a swell gunner," says Lefty. "Any pilot would be lucky to have you at his back."

"Thanks," I growl, feeling a hundred miles from swell. I stare at the underpinnings of Smitty's top bunk. A note is tucked into the wires. I fish it out and swivel around to face The Poet.

"It's from Smitty!"

Rolling over and lifting the mattress, I'm betting that Smitty left us a pack of cigs. But instead there's a fancy postcard set from Ft. Myers Gunnery School flipped open to a picture of an airman reading a poem on a bulletin board. When I see its title, I get so mad I hurl the postcard set across the room.

CHAPTER EIGHT

A Gunner's Vow

Our memory tap ended with a crash. One—probably both—of us had flung the postcard set at the closet doors, knocking over the glass of water on my nightstand. The accordion of paper pictures lay in a heap on my bedroom floor, and water dripped from the tabletop, turning the rug into a wet bog.

"Damn, Sylvie, I'm sorry," said Bish. "I guess we lost the connection."

"Ya think?" I patted at the spilled water with a wadded up t-shirt. I felt pissed, but I wasn't sure why. "It's only some stupid postcards, what's the big friggin' deal?"

"It's 'A Gunner's Vow'," said Bish. "I hated it then, but learned to love it later. Wound up carrying it with me through the whole war."

I read the catchy little poem, knowing then why Smitty left it, and why Bish had hated but saved it.

> *A Gunner's Vow*
> *I wished to be a pilot,*
> *And you along with me.*
> *But if we were all pilots*
> *Where would the Air Force be?*
> *It takes GUTS to be a Gunner*
> *To sit out in the tail*
> *When the Messerschmitts are coming*
> *And the slugs begin to wail.*
> *The pilot's just a chauffeur,*
> *It's his job to fly the plane;*
> *But it's we who do the fighting,*
> *Though we may not get the fame.*
> *If we all must be Gunners*
> *Then let us make this bet:*
> *We'll be the best damn Gunners*
> *That have left this station yet.*
> *—Author Unknown*

"Did you ever find out what happened to Smitty?" I asked, carefully refolding the postcard set.

Bish got up and stared out the window. "I didn't think I'd ever see him again. But maybe two years later, he showed up at Falconara, our new base in northern Italy. Seems he'd been assigned to interrogate German prisoners at a nearby POW camp and to do some air reconnaissance with the 321st."

I thought of how Grandpa Chuck used to interrogate Pen and me at the dinner table about school, plans for the future, pretty much everything. The job seemed to fit. "But after training, where exactly did he disappear to?"

Bish stared into the dark night like he was watching a movie. For all I knew, he was. "MI. Smitty was snatched up by Military Intelligence," Bish said. "We used to joke that his ability to blend in had been noticed."

"Grandpa Chuck a spy?" I asked. He was about 5,000 miles from James Bond in style and action.

"Not everyone in Intelligence is a spy," said Bish. "MI is how we knew where to drop our bombs, where the Kraut strongholds were, what supply lines they relied on."

As he talked, I put the postcards back in their pile on the desk, and picked up one of the engagement pictures.

"That's a story for another time," Bish said, looking first at the picture then at his watch. "I should let you get some rest. We've covered a lot for a first day."

"No shit," I said, snuggling under my covers.

A cold breeze swirled through the partly open window. Bish turned away from me like a guy would if he didn't want anyone to see him cry. For the first time, I saw the painting on the back of his jacket; a plane with two square-ish tailpieces and bubble windows front and tail.

"Nice plane," I said. "How come it's not finished?"

Bish slid a hand into the pocket of his jacket as he turned. He flashed a sad smile. "She's a B-25. Just like the ones we flew. Cooper, our resident artist, got shipped home before he could finish her." He pulled a tiny gray-green plane like the one on the back of his jacket from the pocket. "*Miss Fancy Pants* was my favorite." He smiled and held the plane in the palm of his hand. It was perfect right down to the tiny painting of the topless operator on the nose and the clear plexi-blisters on top and at the tail.

There was something familiar about the jacket and plane, as if they'd wormed deep into my memory. "What happened to it? Your jacket, I mean."

"I asked Smitty to deliver my gear to Merrilee," said Bish, heading toward my bedroom door. "I was dying, I knew it. My guts had been blasted to bits, but all I could think about was how I wanted her to have my gear, everything I'd saved over the years, even my jacket. Smitty promised to take it all to her." Bish's voice slowed and hardened. "Now I find he stole my whole life." He shoved the tiny plane into his pocket.

Tears welled in my eyes and ran down my cheeks as Bish disappeared. Grandpa Chuck had been a good grandfather, someone I'd loved my whole life. But I was torn because I realized he'd never told me the truth. He'd never ever said that he was in our lives because of someone named Bish—because Bish died and Smitty stole his girl.

I was about to click off the bedside light when I heard Grams.

"Sylvie?" She pushed open the door and poked her head into the room. "I thought I heard you talking to someone."

"Sorry Grams, it's just me," I said. "Maybe I was talking in my sleep. Been having weird dreams lately."

Grams came in and sat on my bed. "Tell me about it?"

I bit my lip. What parts of a girl's internal freak show are the right bits to reveal? "It's nothing, really. I dreamed about your Bish guy, that's all."

Grams's face wrinkled with worry. Her whole body tensed. "What about him?"

I ran an index finger over the veins on the back of Grams's hand. "Well," I stalled, looking for the right word in a field of prickly pears. "I was wondering. Is there any chance that Bish guy could be my grandfather?"

Grams's eyes clouded with anger, or was it embarrassment? The air felt heavy, expectant, making me wish I'd never asked. Grams blinked, shook her head. When she finally spoke, she sounded like a zombie. "No, no. Chuck was your Grandpa. Really, Sylvie, what kind of girl do you think I was?"

I shrugged. "One who was in love."

"That makes no difference." Grams patted my comforter and stood. "I was a good girl, Sylvie," she said, her pained face light against the darkness of the room.

Instinct told me she needed me to believe that, to confirm it. "No doubt, Grams," I said. "You're the best person I know."

Grams threw me a weak smile as she bent down to kiss my forehead. "Bish couldn't have a family slowing him down. I even saw the piece of paper from the Air Corps that forbid it."

I ached for her as she clicked off the light on my nightstand and padded down the stairs to her big empty bed.

CHAPTER NINE

NIGHT SHADE

I woke up in the early morning, sweaty and thrashed, happy to be in my yellow room, under my Merimeko comforter. Bish's boys had me freaked, and I scanned the room, worried that they might still be there, lurking. I didn't see anyone, but when I reached beneath the bed for my journal, my hand found it amidst a jumble of Bish's goggles and a dirty t-shirt. Using the shirt as a cleaning rag, I wiped down the thick rubbery rims and clear celluloid lenses of the goggles. The old, black elastic band crackled as I pulled the goggles over my head. My journal crackled as I opened it, too, the pages taking on a weird sort of opalescence. Pencil scratching against journal page, I hid there behind book and goggles as I sketched out that night's dream.

I DREAM OF DEAD GUYS…

They climb out of old photographs
To settle on the end of my bed, sprawl in the side chair,
And lean against the wall.
Good thing some of them are pretty hot
Or I'd have to kick their whiny butts outta here.
They look at me expectantly,
Souls starved by being stuck between worlds.
They pitch their cases, but my ears are made of clay.
Tonight they've invited Mrs. Fenbert,
The toughest teacher in high school.
She taught the tales of ancient escapades,
Of monster quests and major F-ups.
Now she assigns me one last test.
"Chart your hero's journey," she says.
"Find your way along his path."
"Injuste! Not fair!" chorus the guys. "We're heroes too."
"We've launched a thousand ships, hit a million targets."
Mrs. Fenbert says their day will come.
Now it's my time to make a choice, like they once did:

The ding of the doorbell made me jump. I waited, still as a bird in my upstairs room, for Grams to answer. The air seemed thick and foggy, and I could just make out the shape of Bish, asleep on the floor, leaning against the foot of my bed. There was no familiar sound of Grams opening the door, so I tugged off the goggles and threw on my robe, heading downstairs as the bell dinged again.

I opened the door to a smiley-faced lady wearing bright red lipstick.

"You must be Sylvie," she said, cocking her head to one side like a creepy puppet-doll. "I'm looking for Mrs. Merrilee Stevens." She looked past me into the house, so I stepped sideways to block her view.

"Sorry, she's not here just now," I said. "Can I help you?"

"Her daughter Bernadette sent me."

I raised my eyebrows, wondering what Mom was up to.

"I'm Marti Mansfield, seller's agent." She handed me a business card. "Could you please give this to Merrilee?" She held out a packet of papers. "Bernadette said she wanted to go over her options, get some advice on prepping the house for market."

"Oh, really?" I knew Mom had been pushing Grams to move, but I didn't know she'd pushed things so far along.

"There's no time like the present." Marti Mansfield shouldered her way into the entry. "Mind if I take a look around? Bernadette asked me to run some comps. I think with this square footage and fabulous view, we can get a really good price."

I felt a tug on my robe and turned to find Dixon looking up at me. His bright blue eyes were clouded with worry. "Gamma barn," he said. When I glanced downstairs toward the kitchen and family room, Bish and the bomber boys were there, waiting. "Sylvie, you better get down there," said Bish.

"Now's not a good time," I said to Marti Mansfield. "You'll have to come back when my grandmother is here."

"But the little boy said she was in the barn."

I picked up Dixon and he clapped his tiny hands against my cheeks. "Out ick," he said to me, worry in his eyes. He turned to look at the real estate maven. "Out ick."

Marti Mansfield coughed up a prickly laugh. "Well, really."

"I'm sorry," I said, trying not to laugh. "But seriously, now's not a good time. The place is a mess." Opening the door nice and wide, I nodded toward the outside. Marti smiled like a marionette. "Alright then," she said, backing away. "Have her give me a call. I'll give Bernadette a jingle in the meantime." She walked stiffly back to her car, high heels scuffing along the aggregate walkway.

"You do that," I said under my breath. Last I'd heard, Mom had done her thing in Zurich and was somewhere between there and Amsterdam.

I started back up the stairs to my room to get my phone when Dixon squished my face between his little hands. "Seeveee, top," he said. "Out ick."

It finally occurred to me what he was saying. "Oh, my God, Dix. Is that where Grams is? In the barn because Scout is sick?"

He nodded like a crazy guy, wriggled out of my arms, and led me to the barn. The bomber boys crowded in too, and I did a quick scan, relieved that the rest appeared to have stayed in my dream.

When Dixon and I got to the barn, my hand flew to my nose. The stench was gagging. "Grams?" I called.

"In here, Sylvie," she said. I followed her voice to Scout's stall and immediately saw the source of the smell. It was as if someone had literally sprayed the walls with shit. The greenish-brown nastiness had soaked Scout's tail, and it was smeared all over his butt and back legs. The poor old guy must have been heaving his guts out all night.

"Yucky," said Dixon, holding his nose. Scout looked at us with sad brown eyes.

"You go play," I said, setting Dixon down. He dashed out the barn door to the fresh-smelling shavings pile and his toy dump truck.

"Get a lead rope dear," said Grams. "Let's get the old boy out of here."

I unsnapped a blue lead from the ring on the crossties and looped it around Scout's neck. He was wobbly but managed to stay upright as we led him into the fresh air of the pasture.

Gulliver whinnied to his pal and banged against his stall door. When we let him out, he trotted over to Scout, snorting and sniffing, nosing Scout's shoulder until the old boy walked with him to the water trough and took a long drink.

"What's wrong with him, Grams?" I asked, wrapping my arm through hers. My knees were wobbly and my heart hurt. Scout was never sick. "Should we call the vet?"

"I think that's where Kate went," Grams said, not taking her eyes off Scout.

"I'll go check," I said, heading toward the house.

When I passed by the dark, gaping doorway of the barn, Bish was there, a lone figure in the darkness. "Sorry about your horse, gal," he said, looking across the pasture at Scout.

"Wish we could do something," said StuBoy, appearing at Bish's side.

"Why can't you?" I asked, wiping at a tear. "Don't you have some sort of special connections?"

"We're not angels," cut in Valentine, materializing next to me. He leaned a shoulder against the barn wall. A cigarette pack was rolled into the sleeve of his t-shirt.

"Clearly," I said, pressing past, toward the gate.

"We're guides," said StuBoy, trailing after me. "Everybody thinks we can see and do everything, but it ain't so. A fella has to earn his clearance. Most Intel is classified."

"And I'm just a poor SOB trying to make things right," added Bish.

I glanced at him over my shoulder. "Then start by making my horse right."

"I wish it worked that way," Bish said.

"Then what good are you?" I spun around to face them, but not one of them had a reply. Disgusted, I sprinted up the stairs to the house and practically knocked over Kate.

"Doc Weizner is on his way," she said. "Where's Dixon?"

"Shavings bin." I pointed toward the barn. "I'm getting towels and water."

Kate nodded, and as I pushed open the mudroom door, I heard my phone ring. I sprinted upstairs to answer it, praying it was Pen.

"I'll be there in ten," she said when I told her what was going on.

My legs swayed and hands shook as I collected rags and ran hot water into a bucket glopped with shampoo. It felt like the world had become a freakish funhouse, with everything distorted and strange.

Hauling the bucket and towels to Scout and Grams in the pasture,

I stopped for a minute to wrap my arms around Scout's neck. "Oh, buddy, don't die. You can't die. Please don't die. Please be okay." I bit my lower lip and pressed my forehead into Scout's coppery neck.

"Sylvie, honey," said Grams, her hand on my shoulder. "I think he just ate something."

What? My mind wandered through the list of plants Grams always had us pull out of the pasture every summer. Bracken, scotch broom, tansy, buttercup. Could it have been one of those?

"He's the best horse ever," I said.

"You two had a mighty good run," she said. "I remember when you used to win every competition you entered. But the boy is old. You need to be prepared if he doesn't spring back."

"No," I said, refusing to listen. I pulled Scout's lead rope from over his neck and let it fall as a ground tie. He shivered when I poured warm soapy water over his back end and dunked his tail. "I'll get him cleaned up and he'll be fine."

Grams moved silently to Scout's head and rubbed his ears. Crows gathered in a tree at the far side of the pasture.

"You need to put the old boy out of his misery," said StuBoy.

"Listen to him," said Bish. "He knows a little something about horses. Grew up on a ranch."

"Especially if he ate some of that nightshade growing along your fence line." StuBoy pointed to the fence running along a little creek where blackberries had taken over, their vines trailing up the alder trees.

We'd always pulled everything inside the pasture. Hadn't given stuff outside much of a thought. In the last year, Scout had become more and more of a berry hunter since eating hay and grass was so tough. The blackberries weren't ripe yet, but who knew what else was? No, it couldn't be that. StuBoy was wrong.

When Doc Weizner showed up, he did his bit, trying to flush Scout's system. The tube up the nose always got me, but Scout didn't seem to care. As Doc Weizner pumped some kind of magic potion into the old boy, I imagined it just squirting out the other end. It didn't, but it did make Scout wince and convulse with pain. His sides heaved, and his legs began to buckle.

"Keep him up," shouted Doc, quickly retrieving his tube. Grams, Pen and I did our best to keep the old boy standing as a gob of disgusting Jell-Oish black goo blopped out of Scout's butt. Kate held Dixon back and away.

The convulsions eased, but Scout panted like he'd just run a mile flat out. My heart felt like it'd been ripped from my chest.

"What do you think it is?" I whispered to Doc.

"Hard to say," he answered. "I'll know more after I run the fecals." Doc scooped some of the stinky black goo into a small jar.

"What if it's nightshade?" I asked. Everyone looked at me like I was nuts. "I mean, what if there's some just outside the fence and we didn't know it. Like over by the creek."

"Oh, good Lord," said Grams, instantly heading in the direction StuBoy had pointed. Kate and Dixon hurried after her.

"Most horses know better than to eat it," said Doc. "But who knows? Maybe he ate some berries along with something else."

I held Scout as Doc tapped the horse's jugular with a needle and drew blood. Next he injected a painkiller. "That should make him more comfortable. But Sylvie, you should prepare yourself in case he doesn't make it through the night. He's a sick boy. Keep him outside. He'll be more comfortable if he can move around."

What Doc was actually saying was that it's way easier to haul a dead horse out of a pasture than from inside a barn stall.

Swallowing hard, I looked toward the barn. Bish stood framed in the big dark doorway, hands in pockets, eyes on me. Waiting.

I blinked and refocused on Scout and Grams and the big expanse of everything that was safe and familiar. Bish's world seemed so strange and unknown, yet my current one was nothing but pain. My hand gripped Scout's mane.

"When you put a horse down, what happens to the body?" I asked Doc Weizner.

Doc ran a hand along Scout's neck. "Well, some folks bury the animals on site, but that's getting more and more rare. Water table seepage, county rules, and so on. Usually we call in a truck that takes the body to a rendering plant."

Oh, God. "As in dog food?" I said, wincing and putting my hands over Scout's ears.

"And glue, bone meal, and so on." Doc caught my eye. "It's not all bad. Part of the cycle of life."

"Does it cost money or do they pay you for the meat?" I couldn't believe I was asking this, but sometimes in the face of freak-out, my practical side goes into overdrive.

Doc smiled. "Oh, you have to pay alright."

Shivering with the heebie-jeebies, I thought of the bill. Grams already had stacks of overdraft notices and big fat bills from the lawyer's office piled on her desk with too little money to pay them. "How much does all this cost?"

"A few hundred dollars, I suppose," said Doc.

Over by the pasture fence, Kate called out and waved. "We found some." A little creek ran through there and alder trees rose above the blackberries. "We found some nightshade."

"Told you," said StuBoy into my ear.

"Oh, shit," I said, as Scout's sides heaved and his body convulsed again.

DEADLY NIGHTSHADE
Description:
The star-shaped flowers are misleading, all purple and pretty.
Twining on the stems of other plants
It strangles, devours.
Egg-shaped pointed leaves, berries
Are platters of poison for any who dine.

Symptoms:
Confusion, disorientation,
Convulsions that come in waves;
Diarrhea, increased heart rate,
A nervous system under attack.

Treatment:
Eradicate miscreants.
Search them out along fence lines and creek beds.
Strike to the roots with bucket and tube,
Flushing the system with charcoal and electrolytes.
Wait. Watch.
Flush with mineral oil.
Pray, if you dare.
Bargain, if you can.

Demand:
No fuckin' way will you take my horse,
My childhood, my life.

But it does anyway.

CHAPTER TEN

BANK NOTES

The night after Scout was put down and hauled away, he came to me in a dream. I was standing with Bish in front of a big, dark open door when Scout appeared, trotting toward me, metal shoes clicking against pasture stones. He was strong and full of life. His copper coat shone in the setting sun. The old horse searched me for treats as usual, but before I could produce a bucket of bran mash and applesauce, he head-butted me through the doorway into a well of blackness.

Waking up as I fell, I heard Bish. "You should make a *lamella* for him," he said from the depths of the darkness. "Maybe he'll forgive you then."

I struggled to escape the dreamy, dark trap, sheets strangling.

"Guilt can suck the soul right out of you, if you let it." It was Bish's voice again.

"I don't feel guilty." I lied. Blackness swirled around me as if it knew. "I did what I had to do. He was suffering."

"At least that part's true." Bish emerged next to me, ghostly white in the dark fog. "Scout wanted you to help me."

"Really?" I said. "You saw him? He told you that?"

Bish laughed, but it had an edge. "No. That was a cheap shot at getting you back on track. We've got a mission." He looked at his watch.

"Rat bastard. It's day three of twenty-one," I said, feeling slightly creeped out. "Don't think I haven't been keeping track. We have plenty of time." I thrashed against the confining covers.

"Don't be a damn fool, Sylvie," Bish said. He was pacing when I finally freed my head. "Do you know how long it took me to get to Italy? Over a year. Six-hundred-thirty-one days to be exact. And you only have 18."

"For what?" I said, spitting the words as I sat up. I was pissed because he was acting like I was a slacker. If there is a Hell, I was pretty sure the last 24 hours had been it. "You've never even told me exactly what this stupid mission is. Tell me now or just forget it and get the hell outta here."

Bish paused by the deck door and glared at me. "I certainly have told you, and how."

"No, you showed me why you're on a mission, but not what it is."

Valentine materialized on the windowsill. "That's because now that he's here, he thinks it's impossible."

"What?" I said. "What's impossible?" My hands clenched. I would have strangled Bish if he'd been anything more than air.

Bish crumpled onto the other twin bed, head in hands. "We have to find the *lamella*—the tiny golden prayer note the *signadora* on Corsica had me make. Then we have to take it to some church with a deep well in Ala, Italy. We drop the prayer note in there, and supposedly all is forgiven by the little girl and her family. With that forgiveness, everything else is set right." Bish rubbed his face. "But the damn thing is lost."

I thought for a minute, then reached for Bish's goggles. Something had been weird about them. Something I'd missed. I wiped them clean with the bed sheet and slid them over my eyes. The room went three-D for a second until I noticed StuBoy leaning against the deck door. I lifted the goggles. No StuBoy. Goggles on, StuBoy rolling a cigarette. No wonder he was playing Invisible Man. He tried to hide the cig when he realized I'd spotted him. I brushed my index fingers at him in the "naughty, naughty" sign but smiled because he'd already given me an idea.

"Does this *lamella* thing have to be the *lamella*? Can't we just make a new one?" I pushed the goggles up on my forehead to better eyeball Bish. "It's the sentiment that counts, right? You can tell me what was in it. I'll write it down." I was already grabbing the tin foil from the kitchen drawer in my mind.

StuBoy popped into view, cigarette hidden. That's a swell idea," he said, slapping Bish on the back. "I told you she'd come up with something."

"Yeah, real swell," said Bish, pushing his lips together into a frown. "If I could remember. That whole night is a blur."

"So, what about this little girl's family?" I said. "Are any of them even still alive?"

"I always figured I'd just ask around when I got to Ala," said Bish.

"You make it sound so easy," I said. "As if getting there wasn't tough enough. Can't we just use the telephone? Call around?"

"That would cost a fortune," said StuBoy. "Besides they barely have indoor plumbing in those tiny Italian towns. What makes you think they'd have telephones?"

"Dude, it's 2003," I said. "Everyone has a phone." I lifted mine from the nightstand.

"You speak Italian?" Valentine said. "You know the little girl's name?"

Flopping back onto my pillow, tiredness overtook me. "No and no," I said. "But I'm pretty sure I can make a decent *lamella* with a little practice. Let me think on the rest."

It was Bish's day four, afternoon, when Grams and I walked down the road to the sand spit. The bomber boys were on self-assigned escort duty, and I still felt like crap about Scout. At least making a *lamella* for him had made me feel a little better. It was Grams's idea to take it down to throw into deep, gray-green Puget Sound.

Grams helped me fill a little bottle with pebbly sand and Scout's tin foil prayer note. We stoppered it with a rag, hoping the slow seep of water would take it to the deep, deep downs. The sky went gray as I hurled the ancient wish into the chop outside the mouth of the harbor. *Please forgive me Scout.* Grams put her arm around my shoulders and pulled me to her. I couldn't tell if her cheek was wet with her own tears or mine, but it didn't matter. We had both tasted too much loss.

When we finally started home, a crack formed in the clouds and blue sky peeked through. Grams hummed as we walked, and slowly, step by step, the haunting vision of the knacker truck pulling out of our driveway finally dimmed and slipped from my mind. *Please forgive me Scout.*

"Hold out your hand and close your eyes," said Grams, stopping and turning to face me.

I did what she asked, and she placed something hard, cold, and round in my hand. "It's a petrified mint patty," I said.

"No, silly," said Grams. "Open up. It's a wishing rock. See the ring around it?"

A white ring circled the flattish gray stone.

"Keep that with you, and whenever you're sad, just rub it and make a wish." Grams smiled. "And if you need a super-whammie wish, throw the rock over your left shoulder into the water."

I held the stone close to my chest, biting my lip and blinking long and hard. Scout's *lamella* was clear in my mind. First draft scribbled in my diary; second one done for real. It was good practice for Bish's if ever we got there.

> *Dear Scout,*
> *Grams and Bish taught me how to make a* lamella *for you;*
> *A tiny square of tinfoil etched with words*
> *I couldn't keep inside or say out loud.*
> *Bish told me they were secret, sacred*
> *Ancient prayers first carved into gold and lead,*
> *Tossed into wells and over cliffs*
> *To ask forgiveness and bless the dead.*
> *Dear Scout,*
> *Please forgive me for killing you.*
> *Please forgive me for playing God,*
> *For having the vet stop your heart forever.*
> *But there was no way I could*
> *Let you suffer in such pain, or let*
> *The blood-stained knacker man*
> *Put a bullet through the white galaxy*
> *In the middle of your forehead.*
> *Please forgive me for this crappy way*
> *Of thanking you for the pride and courage*
> *You gave to me. I love you and miss you*
> *And hate more than anything having to say good-bye.*
>
> *Sylvie*

"Thanks Grams," I said. I intertwined my fingers with hers and kissed the back of her hand. "It's awesome."

"She gave me one of those rocks too," said Bish. He must have been feeling left out. "I can still see her that time we were at her parent's beach place. She was laughing and smiling, wearing an old blue sweater and dungarees. She had beautiful dark brown hair and the eyes of an imp. And great legs. Did I mention her legs?"

Bish stared at Grams just like he had in their engagement picture.

"Grams, do you ever get the sense that someone you once loved is hanging around?" I asked.

She hesitated, then nodded and shrugged. "Oh, goodness, I don't know. If it weren't for you, I'd feel totally lost all the time. But I have to say, the other night when I couldn't sleep, I swear I felt a hand on my shoulder. Someone was there. Someone trying to console me. For the first time since Chuck died, I felt like someone was watching out for me. After that, I slept like a rock the rest of the night."

I raised my eyes to Bish, but he turned away, no doubt playing innocent.

We were at the last rise of the road home when I noticed a car pull out of our driveway. It wasn't one I recognized. Curious, I stepped up the pace. When we got to the house, nothing looked weird or out of place until I saw a piece of yellow paper taped to the front door. The type was too small to read from where we stood, but I got a weird feeling—like a jellyfish had moved into my gut. When we got to the door, I felt the first sharp sting.

NOTICE OF DEED OF TRUST SALE JULY 11, 2003

Grams stepped up behind me and ripped the paper off the door. "Damn bank," she said. "Everyone wants water from a stone."

"What does this mean, Grams?"

"It means they want to take my house." Her voice was sharp and the paper crackled in her hand as she crushed it.

"Does Mom know?"

"Of course she does," Grams said, sorta melting into the bench near the front door. Bish moved to stand beside her. "Why do you think she wants me to go to that old folks home?"

The text Mom had sent the day before telling me I had to take Grams to see some lady at Grace Retirement Center came to mind.

"Mom said it was because you wanted to have fewer worries," I said.

"Nice way to put it," said Grams. "Chuck struggled for years to keep this place. I can't just let it go to the dogs."

"Didn't he have any life insurance?" asked Bish.

"Didn't he have any insurance?" I asked Grams.

"Oh, sure, he had plenty of insurance over the years." Grams closed her eyes. "But if I understood your mother right, all the policies had been cashed out but one. And that was only about $2,000 dollars. Not near enough to pay off the house."

"Bastard," spat Bish. "I'da never left her in such a piss-poor situation."

I settled in next to Grams on the bench. "How have you been paying the bills till now?"

"Social security. That's how I pay for everything."

Images of overdraft notices piled on Grams's desk came to mind. Clearly Social Security wasn't enough. I worried about the vet and knacker truck bills that Grams had dropped on her desk too. My stomach spun as an idea started to perk.

"You have to help her, Sylvie," said Bish. "We have to help her."

"Don't you ever wish you could run away from it all," I said.

"Sure," said Grams, spinning the vine-inspired wedding ring around her finger. "But where would I go? I can't imagine living anywhere else."

She was shaking, maybe from the cold damp or more likely from the trauma of having her house tagged by the bank gang. I took Grams's hand and led her into the house. The whole deal sucked, but instead of feeling bummed I felt like punching the world back, hard. "If you could go anywhere in the world, Grams, where would it be?"

Bish looked at me like I'd gone nutso, but I really didn't give a shit.

That night, I called Pen to give her the news. "Do you want the good news or the bad news first," I said.

"Good, first, totally."

"Then, the good news is I paid off the vet bills."

"Wow, that's cool, I guess," said Pen. "And the bad?" Her voice wavered a little.

I took a deep breath and let it out. "Well, the bad news is I had to cash in my Alaska ticket to do it." I waited for her to say something, but she didn't, so I floored it. "See, Grams and I came home and there was this foreclosure notice on the house and I remembered the vet bills and I thought, hey she doesn't have any money to pay them, so I had to think of something and it was my fault we had them in the first place because I asked the vet to put Scout down, and so I decided that the only way I could help her was to pay them and the only way I could pay them was to cash in the ticket." I paused to take a breath, but Pen jumped in before I could launch again.

"Foreclosure? Fuck!" she said. "Tell me you didn't say they're foreclosing on your grandmother's house?"

I walked from one side of my room to the other. "I'd love to, but I'd be lying. I texted my mom and she said it was true. Grams is freaked."

"There has to be something we can do," said Pen.

I rubbed the wishing rock in my pocket. "Yeah there is," I said. "We can help Bish with his mission. I have this feeling that if we do that, everything will turn out alright."

Pen sighed. "And we do that how?"

"Well, first I have to figure out where the hell Ala, Italy, is. Second, I have to find the family of a little girl who was killed in the war." The world atlas that was always in Grandpa Chuck's den flashed in my mind. I hoped Fruity Pants hadn't stolen it too.

"Oh, that should be easy," said Pen sarcastically. "No offense, but there were probably hundreds of little girls killed in the war."

"Well, we have to start somewhere."

"What's this 'we' stuff, kemo sabe?" said Pen. "I'm still going to Alaska."

Words stuck in my throat. Surely she hadn't meant to stab me in the gut, but that's how it felt.

CHAPTER ELEVEN

PORTRAITS

"We don't need her anyway," said Bish.

"Tell her I'm gonna dump her if she won't help," said StuBoy.

"I can show you exactly where Ala, Italy is," said Valentine. "Just round up a map."

"I don't mean to be rude, guys, but could you just go?" I reached under the bed for my art journal, opening it to a drawing I'd been working on for a while. "I don't feel like talking." A part of me had really thought Pen would jump on board and stay here with me; the other totally understood why she didn't want to give up her summer adventure.

StuBoy and Valentine moved toward the bedroom door, but Bish stared at the box. He rose to his toes, raised his arms a little, but nothing seemed to happen.

"If you need to move stuff, just ask," said StuBoy. Without a touch, he slid the tiny airplane out of Bish's pocket and sent it loop-de-looping around my room.

Bish caught it mid-air. "And give up on honing my powers of psychokinesis? No sir," he said.

StuBoy shrugged. "What are you after?"

"One of those envelopes of negatives," said Bish.

"You're still lookin' for that bit o' gold, aren't you?" said StuBoy, slapping Bish's arm with the back of his hand. "You've been looking for that since the war was declared finito."

"I thought it might have fallen out of something and into here," Bish said. "You never know."

"All you have to do is focus and lift," said StuBoy.

I heard the splash of negatives on paper and looked over to see an envelope floating upside down in midair.

"That's just swell. You make it look so easy," said Bish.

"I've had lots of practice. Couldn't exactly fix a plane in this state without it, now could I?"

I jumped up and grabbed the envelope, stuffing the negatives back inside. "Would you two quit? What if Grams or Kate walk in?"

"Hang it, Sylvie, these are important skills for a fella to have," said Bish.

"No doubt," I said, setting the envelope on my desk and noticing that the word "Lefty" was written on the envelope's front. "But can't you practice somewhere else?" I slid out a negative and held it to the light.

"There is nowhere else for me," said Bish. He held the perfect tiny bomber plane in the palm of his hand. It levitated for a second, then fell back into his hand.

My heart ached a little for him as I studied the weird reverse image on the negative. It was Lefty all right. He looked a smidge older and wiser than he had in Bish's memory, but it was still him. "Where's Lefty now? Why didn't he show up for your little reunion?"

The boys shook their heads. "He ain't done yet," said StuBoy. "Still hasn't made it to roll call."

"You mean this guy is still alive?" I waved the envelope of negatives at Bish. "Why didn't you say so?"

Bish and StuBoy shrugged. "Didn't know it was important."

"Not important?" My voice cracked with excitement. A living Lefty seemed like just the ticket I needed to determine whether or not I was completely insane. "I've gotta meet him. Where is he?"

"Poe? We haven't been able to locate him yet," said Valentine, appearing in his window seat.

"But you're the radio operator. I thought you were in touch with everybody."

Valentine shook his head. "I can put the call out, but it doesn't mean a fella will answer."

He had a point. But maybe Valentine's form of communication didn't work on the living. "Then I guess we'll have to go looking."

"Looking for what?" said Grams, appearing in the doorway. "Seems like I'm always looking for something, I just can't always remember what it is." She made a goofy face to cover her frustration.

I held up the envelope of negatives marked "Lefty." "Looking for this guy," I said. "Wouldn't it be cool if we could find the guys marked on these envelopes and deliver these sets of negatives to them? It seems like that must have been Bish's plan."

"That'd be quite an adventure," said Grams. She wandered over to the bed where my open art journal rested, pencil set in the gutter.

"Especially since all the rest are dead," said Valentine.

I rolled my eyes at him and moved to close my journal. Grams grabbed my hand. "Goodness dear, that's an extraordinary drawing."

Bish and the guys had nearly vaporized, but they rushed over before I could hide the picture. At first glance, the drawing was a portrait of Scout standing proud and alert in front of the Aspen trees.

"Holy bat balls," said StuBoy. "That's me."

Valentine pointed at another section as a slow smile spread across his face. It was the same smile that was reflected in Scout's coat. The drawing of Scout was composed of tiny portraits of the various bomber boys as I "remembered" them through Bish's memory taps and the pictures in the box. I'd glued some of Grandpa Chuck's old stencil letters on the page to title the drawing "Mind Dump."

Grams slid her glasses into place to get a better look. "Maybe where you really need to be, Sylvie dear, is in art school."

I slammed the journal shut. "Mom would love that. I'm supposed to be a doctor or a lawyer, but, gee, I just can't decide which one."

Grams was good at ignoring my sarcasm. "I once studied sculpture and collage," she said. "I loved art more than anything."

"What made you stop?"

Grams paused. "I used to get lost in sculpting. So lost I stopped wanting to do housework, make dinner, even care for my children. Your mother remembers. I made a lovely sculpture of her."

"What happened to it?" I asked, already knowing the answer.

"I think it must have broken," she said. Her gaze glided over my face as if she was measuring me, mapping me out in clay.

Mom had told me a while back about how Grams and Grandpa Chuck argued like crazy one night when she was little. They yelled so much she pushed the sculpture off the table to make them stop. I couldn't tell if Grams really didn't remember or simply didn't want to.

"I would love to have seen it," I said. "I bet the sculpture was amazing. Why didn't you ever go back to sculpting? You could have, after Mom and Kate were grown."

Grams shrugged. "It never came back. I lost the desire, the ability to get into that creative zone."

Mom had told me how afraid Grandpa Chuck had been that

Grams would leave him for her art. Women do that sometimes.

"I never lost my love of art," said Grams. "Only the ability to make it. But you, you have a gift, kiddo. You should nurture it while you can." Grams rose and wandered to the bedroom door. "Come on down. I'll heat up the teakettle."

I smiled and nodded. "Gimme a few minutes."

Once Grams was gone, I noticed Bish on the spare bed, head in hands. "I'd have encouraged her," he said. "I loved her artsy side. I went to the Museo Vaticano because of her. I prayed beneath the mosaic dome of Saint Apollodorus to be able to see her again." He sighed. "Lotta good that did me."

"Well, technically, old Saint Apollawhatever delivered. You're seeing her now," I said.

"But she's old," said Bish. "A sweet little old lady, but not my girl."

I Frisbeed my journal right through him. "Take that back," I said. "If you'd have lived, I'd be talkin' to an old geezer right about now."

"Touché on that count."

"Plus, she needs you," I said. "She's so lost. Mom thinks that moving her to an old folks' home is the answer."

"Oh, jiminy crackers." Bish adjusted his cap. "That's the last place she probably wants to live. Merrilee grew up in one. Her parents ran a place for old Swedes. I used to have to go sneaking around up there just to see her. Talk about a hundred eyes watching your every move."

I imagined a little old face in every window, watching young Grams and Bish. Hell, I'da kept it secret too.

"I can't imagine Merrilee growing old in a place like that." Bish got up and stared out the window.

"They're different now. Fancier. More social," I said, feeling like Mom's pet parrot. "We're going to see her new place tomorrow. Mom said she could move in as soon as next week."

"That's swell," said Bish, eyeing the box again. "Poor thing. Sure wish I could turn back the clock. Start all over again."

For a second, a little picture floated above the box. "You're doing it," I said to Bish. "You lifted one." Of course the second I said anything and Bish turned to look, it fluttered back into the box. I reached in, curious to see which picture it was.

"It's Merrilee in front of a tent at the beach, isn't it?" said Bish. He turned, smiling.

I nodded and dropped the picture. He didn't even have to tell me that's where they used to make out.

CHAPTER TWELVE

THE NEWSPAPER CLIPPING

"Sylvie, teakettle's hot." It was Grams's voice. I trotted downstairs and through the living room where the top drawer of Grams's antique dresser was open, its contents a jumble. When I got down to the kitchen, I smelled something burning. The back burner of the stove glowed as orange as the outside of the teakettle on it. I tried to lift the kettle, but it was stuck.

"Oh, damn," said Grams, joining me at the stove. "I meant to put more water in there, and now look." She spun the control knob to turn off the burner. "My mind isn't here today."

"It's okay, Grams," I said, putting my arm around her. "Besides, it's a crap-ass teakettle anyway."

"Sylvie, watch your mouth." There were tears in her voice.

"You know it's true, and I can say that because I gave it to you." I laughed and pulled her close. "How about we upgrade to one of those cool electric ones that shut off automatically."

"Brilliant," said Grams into my shoulder. "Then maybe I won't feel like such a damn fool all the time."

"Need some help with the chest in the living room?" I asked. "Looks like you're cleaning it out."

"Oh, I was looking for something, but now I can't remember what it was." Grams made a little half-frown. She looked tired. "Been meaning to clear that junk out for ages."

Uh-huh. "Let's do it then," I said. "Maybe we'll find what you were looking for." I'd gone through enough stuff in that house to know that we'd find a weird combo of junk mail and family treasures.

When we entered the living room, I practically stepped on the atlas. It was open to a big green boot of land. The bomber boys were pushing their case.

"Oh, dear, what's this?" said Grams. She stood above the atlas. "Italy. Bish used to write to me from there."

"Do you know where to find Ala?" I asked, hurking the heavy atlas onto the coffee table.

"It's east of Lake Garda in the north," said Valentine, appearing on the stairs.

I ran my finger over the blue splotches in the northern part—a bunch of lakes.

"Along the Adige River," Bish added, appearing next to me. "A blink or two south of Rovereto. Teenie place. Which is why the Krauts put a supply dump there. Didn't think we'd spot it."

"Car," shouted StuBoy, appearing by the front door.

"It's probably the real estate lady," I said.

Grams glanced at me with one eyebrow raised.

"I heard the gravel crunch," I said, covering. "Aren't you expecting her anyway?"

"It's Penelope," said StuBoy, flashing a pearly-white grin. "How do I look? It's a tough job being a gal's World War II Boyfriend."

I rolled my eyes and shook my head. "You look hot."

"I'll open a window," said Grams, setting down the heavy atlas.

StuBoy frowned and I felt sorry for him. I wondered how it was that such a cutie had died so young.

"Car," called Valentine.

One glance at the black Lexus parked next to Pen's yellow Bug told me this time it was the real estate lady.

Grams and Marti Mansfield went downstairs while Pen came up to the living room with me. She flung herself onto the couch as I started to pick through the junk in Grams's antique chest. "You want help?" she said, smacking her palm against a pair of crazy-print overalls we had scavenged at the Goodwill.

"No," I said. "I want entertainment. Tell me a joke or something. I'm so sick of sorting through old stuff I'm about to scream."

"So stop doing it," said Pen.

"As if that's an option," I grumbled. "I can't stop till Grams moves."

Pen retrieved a piece of paper from my throw away pile. "Oh my god, this is a Gap ad from like 1992. Good thing you saved this."

"Not saving, tossing. Put it in the bag, Ms. Desert Your Best Friend."

"Ow," said Pen. "I thought you wanted me go on without you. It's not like I really want to go by myself, but I'm not sitting around home all summer either."

I stacked a few coasters, tossed old Christmas cards, and set aside some letters addressed to Grams and Grandpa Chuck. "You could at least help me crack this mission deal before you go."

Pen launched into a long rambling set of reasons why I'd never be able to find the little girl's family and why it was futile to even try. I finally pointed to the atlas page to make her shut up.

"What?" she said in response to my finger tapping.

"It's Ala, Pen. The place Bish mentioned. It's real. It's on the map. We could go there."

"What kinda glue you been sniffing?" said Pen. "Us go to Italy?"

"Yeah, why not?"

"I thought you didn't have any money."

"I don't, but who needs money when you have airline miles?" I shrugged and batted my eyelashes. "Mom has so many miles she doesn't know what to do with them."

"Holy shit, girl," said Pen. "My Dad does too. And here I thought you weren't taking this Bish thing seriously."

I stopped listening about then. Shifted my focus to a newspaper clipping in the bottom of the drawer. I wouldn't have thought twice about it, but it showed a picture of Mom all young and happy.

"Earth to Sylvie," said Pen. "I said why do we have to go there? Why not just use the phone?" She was at my side now, leaning over my shoulder. "What's that?"

"Marriage announcement." My tongue stuck to the back of my throat.

Pen whistled. "Oh, baby, check out the Bernadette. But what's with the 'Synokowski' bit?"

"No clue," I said.

I heard Grams and Marti Mansfield by the door. Marti was reassuring Grams that the house would sell soon. She'd had a few bites already. Grandpa Chuck used to tell me about realtorspeak, and Marti had it down. The reassurances, the high-heeled tap-dancing.

I called to Grams when I heard the front door close. Even before she made it into the living room, I handed her the clipping. The paper felt thin and brittle. "I know this is Mom, but why does it say 'Bernadette Synokowski'?" I asked.

Grams studied the clipping. "Oh, dear, that was a long time ago." She sighed. "Didn't you know your mother was married once? She was very young. Too young."

CHAPTER THIRTEEN

THE JACKET

"Whoo, doggies," said StuBoy. "How about a little dose of like-mother-like-daughter?"

"How about a nice cuppa shut-the-hell-up?" said Bish, defending his girl.

My heart beat against my ribs like it was trying to escape. Maybe I didn't know my Mom at all.

"Bernadette was married? No way," said Pen.

Grams shook her head as she gazed at the clipping. "It didn't last long. She ran off with a young boy when she was 17. Mostly, I think, because we weren't too crazy about him. They got married in Reno. Made your grandfather hotter than a bag of red peppers. We only found out because she sent this announcement to the local paper—to spite us." Grams ran her finger over the picture. "Your Grandpa Chuck was right though. The boy was a scoundrel. Ran off with Bernadette's best friend before they'd been married a year."

"Bastard," said Bish.

"No wonder," said Pen.

Pen's right. No wonder Mom's single. No wonder she doesn't trust men. No wonder she worries whenever a guy asks me out.

Grams looked out the window across the harbor. I looked at the newspaper date. May 19, 1962. Mom didn't have me until 1986.

"The whole mess changed your mother forever. Poor thing," said Grams. "She was always independent, but she became obsessed with building a career."

Wheels spun. I wasn't sure whether to be sympathetic or pissed. "So Mom just reinvented herself and got knocked up by some sailor dude when she realized she was going to be old and alone?"

Grams cringed. "Sylvie, don't be so crude. Oceanographer. Your father was an oceanographer, specialized in currents and whatnot."

"Whatever. It's not like Mom ever talks about him."

Grams's hand trembled and the clipping crackled with the movement.

"Your mother was heartbroken after all this marriage business. She took the car and drove and drove. I don't even know where all she went. Chuck and I wanted her to come home, but she wouldn't have it. She headed east and never came back. Until you were born."

Grams put her hand on my arm. "Then, lucky for us, her travel schedule took off and she needed us to take care of you in the summers." Grams brushed the stray bangs out of my eyes.

"Your mom never told you any of this?" Pen asked. Her mouth gaped like a goldfish.

"She doesn't tell me a lot," I said, putting my head on Grams's shoulder.

"Poor little gal," I heard Bish whisper to the boys.

Grams sighed. "She and your grandfather were a lot alike. Never wanted to talk about certain things." Grams gazed across the room as if she might find her memories beyond the living room window. "Chuck used to get so angry when the girls asked about the war. He about burst a gasket when he found the girls trying on his bomber jacket."

"That's because it wasn't his," said Bish.

"All they wanted to do was wear it to show and tell." Grams went on. "Bernadette was doing a report for school. Wanted to tell the world what a hero her father was."

"Who wouldn't?" I glanced at Bish, dying to ask him more, but not wanting to freak out Grams.

Bish flashed a weak smile. "I never told Smitty about the *lamella*. I kept it in a secret pocket in the lining of my jacket, waiting for the day I could deliver it."

"Bernadette took the bomber jacket when she ran away," said Grams, pointing to the picture.

I hadn't noticed the leather jacket slung over her shoulder in the 1960s glam shot that served as her wedding announcement.

"Chuck swore like nobody's business when he saw that. Even threw a plate against the wall. Scared little Kate to tears."

"So Mom still has the jacket?" I asked, my cheery picture of Grandpa Chuck officially beginning to warp.

"Who knows?" said Grams.

I glanced at the newspaper clipping again, took in the photo of Mom as a skinny, pretty, hippie. A white halter-top dress. Long, dark wavy hair. White go-go boots. A jacket thrown over her shoulder.

"Something old," I whispered, reciting the opening of that ancient bridal rhyme. "We gotta get that jacket."

"It won't do us any good even if she did still have it," Bish said. "It's gone. The *lamella* is gone."

So you say, I thought, sliding my phone out of my back pocket.

"Syl, it's just an old jacket," said Pen. "What's the biggie?"

"It was Bish's, I know it."

Grams frowned at me as I typed a text message to Mom. Within two minutes the phone buzzed.

"Yes why?" Mom replied.

"School project," I texted back.

"Liar."

"Grams wants it."

"Gray box top shelf. Don't forget to take GM to Grace. It's right nearby."

"Got it." I snapped my phone shut. "Okay, people. We're going to Seattle."

The next morning, it took us less than an hour to get to our Alki Condo. Grams, Pen, the bomber boys, and I rummaged around Mom's perfectly organized closet looking for gray boxes. There were exactly 13 of them. Nine were shoeboxes. Three held sweaters. One was big and flat. I went for that one.

"Oh, my," said Grams when I opened the box. "It's been so long I'd forgotten what it looked like."

"Sweet!" said Pen as I slid on the jacket and looked at myself in the mirror.

"Imagine that," said StuBoy.

"I can't believe they kept that old thing," said Bish. "Musta worn it a load too."

"That's love," said Valentine, leaning against the doorframe, arms crossed.

The jacket in the mirror was cracked and worn, the designs on its patches barely visible. It surprised me because the jacket Bish was wearing—weirdly, this jacket—seemed practically new in comparison. Then I realized that the one I had on was 60 years older and worn who knows how much by Mom.

I ran my finger over a rectangular patch just below the collar.

Bish was right. It wasn't Grandpa Chuck's coat. 'Bishop' was stamped there plain as my face in the mirror. Bish stood behind me, and for a second we looked like boy-girl twins. Same wild, curly blond-brown hair. Same height. Same eyes. Same jacket. I pushed my hands into my pockets and grinned. Bish got that I was copying him and smiled. Same dimple, right cheek.

Bish reached for my sleeve. Warmth swirled up my arm, through my body.

"This needs re-stitching," said Grams, picking at a round patch showing an eagle carrying a bomb in its claws.

Bish and I lost the connection and snapped back to the now.

I shook my head and peeked at the inside of the coat. The little heart patch was still there, but the lining was worn and torn at the bottom where the patch stitching had come undone.

"I made that for Valentine's Day," said Grams, reaching for the tiny heart.

"She sent it in a letter," said Bish.

"We used to kid Bish about it," said StuBoy.

"Only because we all wished we had sweethearts as true as Merrilee," said Valentine. He pinched the bridge of his nose and turned toward the doorway. He'd definitely been burned.

While they were all floating down Memory River, I frisked the coat. How could the *lamella* just disappear? "It has to be here somewhere," I muttered.

"I told you," said Bish. "It's gone."

"What?" said Pen.

"The *lamella*, Bish's prayer note thingy," I said. "The one I'm supposed to deliver. I really thought it would be here. This is friggin' impossible."

"Nothing is impossible," said Grams, unaware of the bomber boys, but, as ever, encouraging me.

I squinted and breathed in the old leathery smell of Bish's coat. StuBoy had a point. "But how am I supposed to know what the message is if I can't find the *lamella*?"

"That's a cinch," said Bish. "I'll show you." He reached out to touch the coat again, but Grams unknowingly intercepted him and wrapped her arms around me.

"Seeing you in that coat brings back such memories."

"Really?" I said, surprised that she remembered anything about it at all. "Such as?" She looked like she was going to cry, but I totally wanted to know anyway.

"All I knew was that Bish was somewhere on Corsica," said Grams. "There were posters everywhere telling people not to say a word about where our boys were. 'Loose lips sink ships' and all that. When we exchanged letters all he wanted was news from home, but I couldn't tell him everything." Grams ran her hand down the sleeve of the coat, over another patch painted with the American flag. "Mostly this coat makes me think of all the hours I sat on the beach wrapped in it because I missed Bish so much after he'd been killed. I wanted to die too."

Grams closed her eyes. Bish reached out and put a ghostly hand on her shoulder, put his forehead ever so gently against hers. I wanted to know more about how he died, too, but right then was so not the time to ask. Instead, Pen and I looked at each other. I glanced at StuBoy and Valentine, and we all backed quietly away to give them a moment. Life—and death—is so unfair. They should have been together.

I slid off the jacket and put it back in its box. It may not have the hidden *lamella*, but the jacket still kept its share of secrets.

My phone dinged, reminding me that we were supposed to be down the road in fifteen.

"Guess we better get down to that Grace place," Pen said, nodding toward the door.

Bish faded. Grams opened her eyes and straightened her coat. "How about we go jump off a bridge instead?" she said. Her delivery was so deadpan I couldn't tell if she was really kidding.

As we walked into Grace Retirement Community, I realized that Grams had to come to Italy with me. She was the ultimate cover. But more than that, I wanted to help her escape Mom's crazy-ass plan—at least for a while. I had no idea how I'd pull it off, but I couldn't believe Mom and Kate signed Grams up for this place without her even knowing. The only good things about it were that it was close to our condo, it appeared clean and neat, and so far didn't smell like pee.

"Your daughter Bernadette picked out a very nice unit for you." The round, smiley leasing lady wore a name badge that said, "Olive Anderson."

"Oh, she did, did she?" said Grams, flashing what I knew was a fake-o smile. I squeezed Grams's hand.

"Oh, goodness yes," said Olive. She put a key in a lock and pushed open an apartment door. "Number 113 has a lovely patio, its own bedroom, bathroom, even emergency pulls in case you fall or need help of any sort."

"That's nice," said Grams, looking around the well-worn apartment. It had barfy mauve colored walls and 1970s dark brown cabinets. It was so not her sky-lit kitchen and master bedroom with a killer view.

Pen slid open a glass door and stepped onto the patio. "Mrs. S, you gotta see this!"

I followed Grams, and Pen pointed us toward a set of garden plots. The one at the end was filled with sunflowers.

"They're beautiful," said Grams.

"Many of our residents enjoy gardening," added Olive.

"I have a big garden at home." Grams crossed her arms like she wasn't interested in gardening anywhere but in her own private weed patch.

Olive must have been used to this awkward resistance because she ushered us back into the apartment and toward the door. "How about I give you the grand tour?" she said.

Grams glanced at me with haunted eyes, like she was an innocent prisoner being shoved behind bars. I squeezed her shoulder.

"This place is for old people," she whispered to me. I laughed but wasn't sure if Grams was kidding. No doubt when she thought of Bish, she was back to being seventeen.

We followed Olive down the long hallway flanked by twenty-billion doors that all looked the same. The bomber boys apparently decided to use their powers of "poof" to look into each apartment to see if they could find Lefty. "He was from Seattle," said Bish as he stepped through a door.

I tapped a nameplate on a nearby door that said Zori Carovich. "These name plates are great," I said, hinting to the boys so they'd realize they didn't have to go spying on old people. "So much better than anonymous numbers."

Valentine poofed back into the hall in front of Olive Anderson. "Darned old naked guy nearly dusted me," he said.

Olive stepped through Valentine and he let out a howl. Bish and StuBoy appeared in the hall, laughing. I snorted and Pen elbowed me. She could no doubt tell by the look on my face that the boys were up to something. "Olive," I said, trying to ignore the boys. "Do you know if anyone named Leonard Allyn Poe lives here?"

Olive pressed a manicured index finger to her Mrs. Claus cheek. "Oh, dear, I know just about everyone here. Poe? I don't believe so. At least not in the apartments."

We rounded a corner into wheelchair central. It was a whole different universe here than in Apartmentland. Lopsided old folks were parked in the halls or wheeling slowly along like giant metallic-wheeled snails. Bent forward, with legs inching along, they seemed to carry their whole lives on their backs.

"This is our rehab unit and care center," explained Olive. Nurses looked up from their half-moon shaped station. "And just beyond these doors is the Memory Care unit." Olive pushed open a metal swinging door. A bright yellow, plastic barrier hung across the entranceway. "It's a wander guard for some of the more active residents," explained Olive. She smiled and lifted one side of the yellow barrier off a hook.

"Looks like jail to me," said Grams under her breath. She took in the group of old fogies parked in the sitting area. One clutched a plastic baby doll. One dozed beneath a blanket, frown lines etched in her toothless face. One yelled obscenities and demanded to call her daughter. Bells dinged and buzzers buzzed. A thin, bug-eyed woman sat silently shredding tissues.

Grams turned and pushed back through the metal doors. Olive trotted after her. "Didn't you want to see the rooms?"

"I've seen plenty," said Grams, bee-lining to the main lobby.

"Then all we have left is a little paperwork," said Olive. "Your daughter has already paid the deposit, so all that's left is your monthly rent, which your social security should mostly cover."

"Well, isn't that nice," said Grams. She was too polite to say, "Fuck this!" like I knew she wanted to.

Olive smiled. "It'll be all ready for you when the movers bring your things next week." Olive worked her way through what seemed to be a mental checklist. "Saturday, I believe your daughter said."

I nodded, dodging Grams's eyes. Kate even had a U-haul truck reserved. Her husband Carter and I had been lined up for moving duty. What a bunch of traitors.

Once we were settled in the car, Grams burst. "Why doesn't your mother ever listen?" I'd never heard Grams sound so miserable and desperate.

"I've been wondering that my whole life," I said, buckling my seat belt. "She only hears what she wants to."

"I don't want to live in that place. So what if I'm a little forgetful. Can't we just buy a little house and I'll live there? You can live with me."

My heart ached. "Grams, we don't have any money. If we did, we'd buy back the big house." The foreclosure sale loomed large on our calendar. Mom said it was for the best—the only way to get the bloodsuckers off Grams's case. But it seemed so unfair. The whole world seemed unfair.

Grams pretended to forget about her lack of money, but I knew it was a front. It was her way of blocking out the realization that Grandpa Chuck left her in such debt, so homeless and destitute.

"Things aren't all bad," said Bish. He and the boys were crowded around Pen in the back seat. "Now we're cleared for Italy. Fifteen days and ticking."

He had a point.

"Maybe we should skip town." I caught Bish in the rearview mirror.

Grams sighed. "Sure would beat growing old in that place."

"How about Italy?" said Pen. "We could lounge around on a nice Italian beach."

"Drink whole bottles of wine," said Grams.

Pen laughed. "Eat a different flavor of gelato each day."

"We could go to Ala," I said.

"And Rovereto," said StuBoy.

"Shop for fancy shoes in Milan," added Pen.

"Find Maria Dolens," said Valentine.

"Swim in the Mediterranean," said Grams.

"Find all the places Bish visited," I said.

"That would be magic." Grams's eyes gazed out over the Narrows as we crossed the big green bridge. It was great to see her smiling again.

"A most excellent plan," said Pen. "All we need is money."

I peered over my sunglasses and eyed Pen in the rearview mirror. "Or miles."

"And the *lamella*," said Bish.

"And the *lamella*," I echoed.

Group optimism always makes things seem so possible. But for all the great plans we made during the ride home, nothing made it seem more important and impossible than what came next.

GRANDMA LOST THE CAR TODAY

The firemen found her wandering and confused.
They gave her a ride home in their big red truck,
Thankful for the address on her driver's license.
The doctor is annoying with what he won't say—
Calls it Short Term Memory Loss.
Grandma says it's just a little case of CRS: Can't Remember Stuff.
I say it's grief—
The sadness and guilt that comes when you're haunted
By your husband's death, the one you blame yourself for.
"I should have made him go to the doctor sooner," said Grams.
"I picked the wrong hospital."
They had revived Grandpa Chuck twice.
The third time his heart was done.
Done trying to make a million. Done living his buddy's life.
Done fighting with the government over land that
   never shared his dream.
After a forty-two year roller-coaster ride of boom and bust,
How could Grams feel she'd failed him?
It makes my heart hurt just to think
How he left her wandering, lost, alone.

CHAPTER FOURTEEN

CINQ FRANCS

"Maybe it was because she never stopped loving Bish." I looked up from my journal to find Valentine, arms crossed, reading over my shoulder. It'd been two days since we visited Grace Retirement Center and Grams had gone into a tailspin. The afternoon sun had disappeared, leaving my room in shadow.

"People go crazy with lost-love and regret all the time," he said.

"What are you, some kind of love doctor," I asked, sketching in a broken heart.

"Nah, just been there." Valentine moved over by the box and bent close to look at some of the pictures I'd pulled out and placed on the desk.

"Ain't that the truth," said Bish, appearing next to Valentine. "Folks think it's only the living that hurt. Boy, they sure got that wrong." He parked it on the bed next to me, looking at my journal. "Hey, that's my money," he said.

He'd spotted the five francs note I'd found in the box and was using as a bookmark. "Prove it," I said.

"Don't be a twerp," said Bish. "They gave us money when we shipped out to Corsica. I kept it as a reminder."

"Of?" I asked.

"Of the people," said Bish. "See, it has a shepherd on one side and this *signadora*-looking gal on the other."

We both reached for the bill and held.

"If it hadn't been for that little old *signadora*, I'd probably still suffer from the evil eye. Sure as hell wouldn't have made the *lamella*."

"Really?" I said, baiting him. My fingers grew warm and tingly and the *cinq francs* note went weirdly 3-D. The colors pulsed and the flowers on it bloomed. I tried to focus on the picture of the lady, but instead I was sucked through time and found myself slapping the bill on a bar made of ration crates. The class ring was on my finger, clue #1 that I'd stepped into another of Bish's memories.

"Franco, give me another," I slur. I'm in the camp club, where an old fella plays the accordion, glasses clink, voices blur.

"You need sleep," says Franco. He's Corsican with dark eyes, a thick mustache and a nose as big as a bomber wing. He knows the ways of the island. "Go home. You no be out when spirits walk and *mazzeri* run."

"What does it matter?" I pound a shot glass on the bar. "I might as well be dead." Images of that tiny girl haunt me. She could have been my little sister. My daughter.

I cough and wipe spit off my lower lip. Warm air. Sand. The scirocco winds swirl through the club—a canvas tent staked at the edge of the island. We're stuck on this island of dream-hunters—the *mazzeri*—mystics who hunt in their sleep and see those destined to die. We boys try not to guess which ones of us they see.

I scratch my head; finger the grit. "Why do good folks die and bad men stay alive?"

"C'est le destin," says Franco, taking my glass.

"You and your Corsican voodoo." I slide off the stool and drift like Sahara sand in the scirocco toward the door.

Outside, in the dark night, a giant moon hovers. Frogs sing back-up to the fading accordion. Tents are quiet, boys rest in anticipation of a morning mission. I shiver and spit out the rancid taste of being declared unfit for duty.

I want to get the hell out of here. So I run, stumbling at first, then faster, steadier—past my tent, past the mechanics' sheds, past Benson's darkroom, past the tip of runway, and out onto a road that snakes up, up into the hills. I pound through the scrubby *maquis* and wild olives, past menacing eucalyptus trees. My lungs burn with their sour scent.

Fingers clench and release with each stride, still wondering how they could have pulled the trigger; why they hadn't stopped the bullets. They're murderer's hands now.

Merrilee would hate me for being a kiddie killer, for not being an officer, for losing my nerve. What would our children think if they knew? How could I ever tell them? My stomach churns into a ball of barbed wire. I don't ever want to tell.

I stop, not caring about staying alive. Teetering on the edge of a cliff, I laugh at Death. *"C'est ma destinée!"* I shout into the night.

My feet turn back from the cliff and run on till the road
dead-ends at a makeshift square. It's a shepherd's perch of
rock-faced sheds, where hay spills from a bricked-up boul-
der, and a lone ewe stands picking and munching.

I trip on a hay-covered ledge and fall into darkness. My
lungs burn.

I, Sylvie, wanted out of that twisted memory. I didn't like this
Bish. But my hand wouldn't let go of the *cinq francs* note. Struggling
got me nowhere in a body I didn't own. Instead I smelled hay and wet
wool; and opened my eyes to a black-faced sheep.

"You go," the sheep insists. No, not a sheep, a woman,
standing over me, shaking me with a black-shoed foot.

"Go back, the *mazzeri* still hunt."

I try to sit up but can't get a firm base in the hay. When
I finally roll to my stomach and sit up on my knees, sparks
dance through my vision.

A rock wall steadies me. My hand grasps a pounding
head. "Who are you?" I ask.

"Signadora," says the woman, assessing my trembling
hands, my rumpled uniform. Her wrinkled face is kind and
her lavender scent comforting, like she's been around since
time began.

"Signa-what?" I say, blinking the sleep out of my eyes.

"Signadora," the woman repeats, eyeing me with concern. She looks into my eyes, reaches out to still my hands.
Her touch is cool, firm. "You suffer," she says. "I help." She
releases me, but motions for me to follow.

"Doing fine," I say, struggling to stand, catching myself
against the rock wall.

The ewe butts me. The woman shakes her head. The
black scarf draped over her head and shoulders flutters in
the warm breeze. "Evil eye make sick," she says, motioning
to me again.

I cringe, unable to admit just how much I ache and hate
myself. Thankfully, her English is spotty. The fewer words
the better. Muscles tight from my crazed run, I stumble after
the *signadora,* across the stone-paved village plaza. She steps
through a doorway and pauses for me to catch up. When I
do, she moves inside and points to an old, wooden table and

chairs. *"Asseyez-vous,"* she says. "Sit."

Chair legs scrape against stone as I settle at her command. White-washed stone surrounds me. Herbs hang on wall racks, their scent making me dizzy when I breathe. The hollow sound of sheep hooves on stone floor echoes in the tiny house. It's the black-faced sheep that woke me, heading for a straw bed by the hearth.

"Angelina, she bring news of you," says the woman, motioning toward the ewe. "She worry."

I snicker. "A sheep?"

The *signadora* raises her eyebrows, suggesting that I'm ignorant to the intellect of sheep. She sets a wide, shallow bowl of water in front of me. It makes me realize how thirsty I am, so I put my hands to its rim and lift it to drink.

"Non!" The *signadora* shakes her head. "Not for drinking," she says, making the sign of the cross before settling in opposite me.

Not for eating, either, obviously. I'm even more confused when she lifts a small bowl of olive oil to a stand above a candle, says some sort of long-winded prayer, and dips her left pinky finger into the oil. Three drops slide from her little finger into the bowl of water in front of me as she makes the sign of the cross again.

"What the hell kinda nonsense is this?" I say.

The *signidora* gives me such a fierce look that I freeze, only rotating my eyes to watch the oil disperse into thousands of tiny droplets floating on the water.

"Is very, very bad." The *signadora* lets her eyes fall half-closed as she whispers a chant and prods at the oil blobs. None of them stick together. She taps her forehead, her chest, her left breast then right. Another sign of the cross. "The evil eye has strong hold," she says. The lines on her face seem deeper. "We do again."

She collects the bowl from the table and tosses the water out the back window into the *maquis* bushes. I sit with my head in my hands, and before I know what's what, the old woman slices off a lock of my hair and places it on the table. "What the hell?" I howl, trying to stand and get the hell out of there.

The old woman pushes me back into the chair with amazing strength, and places the bowl of water on top of my lock of hair. She takes my hands, places them around the bowl's rim. Again, she makes the sign of the cross before dipping into the hot oil and letting three drops slide from her pinky into my water bowl. She whispers some ancient and mysterious French—who knows if it's a curse or a prayer—as she dips her index finger into the water bowl to chase the drops like a mother duck rounding up her brood.

She isn't ugly, I think, studying her features in the lamplight. Old and slightly sad, but not ugly. In fact, there's a sort of radiance about her, but I can't tell if it's the type a fella should fear or admire. Probably both.

The *signadora* grunts and frowns. The oil isn't cooperating. She makes the sign of the cross and tosses the water into the *maquis* again.

Two more times she fills the water bowl, makes the sign of he cross, whispers incantations in forgotten French, and dribbles three drops of hot oil into the water. By the fourth time through the ritual, she smiles a tiny smile.

"What does it mean?" I ask, now so entranced by the process I'd stopped trying to get away. The ewe rests by the fire chewing her cud.

"You fight *destinée*, soul break," says the *signadora*, making the sign of the cross.

"What does that mean?" I ask, but she slips into some sort of trance and is prodding the oil blobs again. This time they are still separate but many have formed alliances with other blobs in the bowl.

On the fifth time, the *signadora* holds the bowl over my head and lets the oil drops fall slowly into the water. When she sets the bowl on the table in front of me, I see that the drops, instead of scattering into a hundred tiny droplets, have become one large mass.

"It is gone," she says. As the *signadora* tosses the water and oil into the *maquis* bushes one last time, I realize I'm starving. I haven't felt hungry for days. She turns a smiling worn-toothed face to me. "Do not fight the *destinée*. When you do, the evil eye take hold. Your heart very, very black. I saw what made it so. The *mazzeri* have seen so many since you English came here."

"Seen so many what?" I ask.

"Dead men." She sets a small loaf of bread and a wedge

of cheese on the table in front of me. *"Mangez.* Eat. Then you finish."

I stuff the bread in my mouth and alternate between bits of bread and cheese. "Finish?"

The *signadora* comes back to the table with a scrap of paper-thin gold not more than two inches square. "Write prayer of pardon." She makes an indent in the gold with the eye-end of a bone needle. "You. Now."

At first, I have no idea what to write, but then I think of the little girl, and what the *signadora* has said begins to sink in. After I press the first word into the gold, the rest tumble and swirl into the air, mixing with the soft sweetness of the ewe's herby breath.

The *signadora* extinguishes the flame below the olive oil and pushes back her single window curtain to let in the day. When I'm done writing, she says simply, *"Plissez,"* pointing at the tiny piece of gold and miming a fold with her fingers.

I do as I'm shown, folding the tiny prayer sheet in thirds then rolling it like a cigarette.

The *signidora* picks up the tiny prayer note, touches it to her heart, and presses it into my hand. *"Preghiera,"* she says, curling my fingers around the prayer. Her touch makes me think of Merrilee.

"Now you must take to place you did wrong. The eye it go then, for always. Everything make right."

My mind spins. How I'll ever get to Ala in this war is beyond me, but I know I have to try. As I rise to leave, "I will," tumbles from my lips. The *signadora* takes my hand, pushes open her old wooden door, and leads me into the daylight. *"Merci,"* I say.

When she let go, I was back in my room with Bish sitting across from me on the bed. "Whoa, that was trippy," I said, reaching for the *cinq francs* note that had fallen to the floor. "What time is it?" It felt like I'd been gone for days.

"Same time your time," said Bish, getting up as if to leave. "Memory taps take place in another dimension."

I yawned. "Seriously?" I flopped on my bed and rolled into my comforter, then sat up in a hurry when the memory came flooding back. Reaching beneath my bed, I grabbed my journal and flipped it open.

Bish got up and moved toward the door. "Where are you going? Don't you see that we've got it now?" I said, transcribing the words Bish had etched into gold onto my journal page so that they didn't escape. As I wrote, Bish's second worry wormed its way back into my mind.

"Is it true?" I asked.

"Is what true?" said Bish, pausing at the door.

I bit my lower lip, uncertain how he'd respond.

"Was she? Was Grams—Merrilee—pregnant with your kid?"

Bish gulped and dug his hands into his pockets. "What difference does it make?"

"I need to know."

Bish stepped back into my room. "Look Sylvie, if you have to know," his voice was hesitant, "Merrilee and I were only together one night. One night before I shipped out. She didn't want anyone to know."

Bish closed his eyes. His face contorted as if he was in pain. "She was only seventeen."

I bit at a hangnail to quiet my shaking hands. "So I should call that a 'yes'?"

Bish shook his head. "I wish I knew. Only Merrilee knows for sure."

Air slid between my teeth in a soft hiss. "Is that really why you're here?" I asked. "To find out if you had a kid?"

Bish looked at me with hurt eyes. "No. I wanted a life with Merrilee. To have children, to grow old together. But I pissed away that chance by not doing what the *signadora* said. I meant to deliver the *lamella*, I even did some recon on where. But I put it off so long I wound up dead." He turned to go.

"But if we do this thing, if we deliver the prayer note and ask for forgiveness, everything gets set right?"

Bish nodded. "Supposedly that's the deal. We can't know the particulars, but yes. Everything between then and now gets set right."

Images of Grams's face during our visit to the Grace memory care unit swam through my mind. The scared eyes of a little girl. Bish's agony under the evil eye. Mom treasuring an old bomber jacket. It was all part of me and was slowly beginning to make sense.

I pulled my phone out of my back pocket. "Award reservations," I said when the line connected. "International."

CHAPTER FIFTEEN

POE'S NEGATIVES

"How's your Italian?" I said to Pen when she showed up at the house the next morning. The fake emerald glued to the middle of her forehead and the crazy, big, dangly earrings that hung above her loose sunflower-covered shirt were a whole new kinda fashion statement.

"Nil to shitty," she said, following me up to my room.

The boys and I had been pouring over the map of Italy in the atlas I borrowed from Grandpa Chuck's den. She looked at it and saw that I'd marked the tiny town of Ala. "Oh, Syl, you didn't."

"Oh, yes I did," I said. "Cash in your Alaska ferry ticket and come with us. I already made you a reservation."

Pen blinked. "Huh? But how?"

"Mom's account had like 350 bajillion miles. We only need 50,000 each round trip plus hotels." I put my hands on Pen's shoulders. "It's a total score."

"And she's okay with that?"

"She'll never know the difference."

Pen blinked. "Seriously? The all-seeing Momclops?"

I glanced at Bish and the boys. They all gave me the thumbs up. "Hey, you're the one who always says it's easier to ask forgiveness than permission."

"That's for little stuff, Syl," said Pen. "This is huge."

"Yeah, well, get over it because Grams and I are going. The bomber boys too." I pointed to the atlas page. "We leave for Milan day after tomorrow. Are you in?"

Pen looked to the ceiling and crossed herself. Walked around the room. Stopped at the box and looked at all the pictures of the bomber boys lined up on the desk. She picked up the picture of StuBoy and kissed it. "Okay. Yep. Oh my god, we're so toast. But yeah, I'm totally in." She wrinkled her face into a worried-but-excited-frown that popped the fake emerald right off her forehead.

"Hot diggety," said StuBoy.

"I knew you'd come round," I said, smiling. "And StuBoy is pumped."

"He's here?" said Pen.

"They're all here," I said with a shrug.

"Always?" Pen looked at me sideways.

"Well, not when I pee or change clothes or anything like that."

Pen looked relieved. "Good, because I'm not going anywhere with Peeping Tom spirits."

"Hey! We're gentlemen," said StuBoy, playacting at being offended.

"She's like a little sister," said Valentine.

"Don't let her derail you," said Bish.

I picked up the envelope of negatives. "Now that you're on board, we have to find Poe."

"Why him?" Pen asked.

"Because a) we have to deliver these negatives to him like Bish originally meant to," I said, waving the envelope at Pen. "And b) he's the only living person who can verify Bish's story."

"What's this? All of a sudden you don't trust me?" said Bish. He crossed his arms and wrinkled his forehead.

"She was raised by old Smitty," said StuBoy, elbowing Bish. "He never took anybody's word for anything."

Valentine looked up from the atlas. "Don't listen to these jackdaws, Sylvie," he said. "We've got orders to find Poe too."

I turned to him. "You do?"

Valentine nodded. "That's the part Bish didn't spill. According to Headquarters, in order for this mission to fly, we have to assemble the whole crew."

"Seriously?" I said, falling back onto my bed, deflated. "We have to find the whole crew?"

"It ain't all that bad, Little Syl," said StuBoy.

Pen picked up the crew photo. "You know how much I hate it when you all have a conversation without me. Especially when I know the next second you're gonna be beggin' for my help."

"It's not like I can help it," I said.

"So it's these three guys in the top row we have to track down?" Pen pointed to the crew photo. "Let me guess—pilot, co-pilot, and...."

"Bombardier," said Bish. "Feinstein was the bombardier. Got stuck in the nose. Poor fella."

"Bombardier," I repeated, feeling more than ever like I was in a game of Password.

"Rounding them up shouldn't be too tough," said Valentine. "At last report, Feinstein and Naussman had been sent in for escort."

"Feinstein and Naussman are with Poe?" I repeated, both for myself and Pen. "But I thought they were dead." The realization of what this meant flooded my head. "Oh, crap, we gotta hurry."

"But we still have no clue where Poe is," said Pen.

"Might start with a telephone book," said Bish.

"Or a military record," said Valentine.

"Or a letter," added StuBoy.

"We don't have any letters in here from him," I said, running my hand through the box and eyeballing Bish. "You didn't even write his name in your address book. What gives?"

"We were stationed together," said Bish. "Who writes letters to buddies you're stationed with?"

Pen pulled out her phone. "Let's 411 him. How many Leonard Poes can there be in Washington?"

I shrugged. "And if that doesn't work, we can Google him," I said before remembering that Grams had no computer, no Internet. We'd even canned the milk and paper deliveries.

The bomber boys passed each other puzzled looks. "Sounds kinda fun," said Valentine. "Come here, StuBoy, I want to Google you."

"Get the hell off me," said StuBoy, smacking Valentine with his hat. The boys laughed and messed around until Bish chimed in.

"Well, whatever it is, you better hurry it on up. We're down to 5 days."

"Get me something to write with, quick," Pen said. She was already talking to the 411 auto-assistant. "There's only two. Better hope one of them is him."

After a couple of hours and a bunch of phone calls, we finally found Lefty in the assisted living section of Sahalie Point. "It's not that far from here," said Pen.

We managed to get old Leonard "Lefty" Poe on the phone and asked him if he'd talk to us. "Sure enough," he said between coughing fits. "But you girls best get down here sooner rather than later. I never know if I'll make it another day."

"We'll be there in an hour or so," said Pen as I gathered up the negatives and photos.

When I knocked on Lefty's door, there was no answer.

"Maybe he's out golfing or lounging by the pool," said StuBoy. "This place is plenty swank."

I knocked again.

"Come on in!" Lefty rumbled and wheezed. "Everyone else does."

Pen and I tiptoed into his apartment. The boys followed.

"Hi Mr. Poe," I said. "It's me, Sylvie Stevens. And this is my best friend, Penelope Jones. We talked to you on the phone about Keith Bishop, the tail gunner."

Poe squished his lips together into a rumpled frown, looking a lot more like a "Leonard Allyn Poe" than a limerick-reciting "Lefty." "Sure, that's right," he said from his recliner. He clicked off the TV and set the remote on a little table to his left. "We trained together. Cocky little fella." Lefty rocked a couple times and managed to stand with the help of a walker. He was still a Jimmy Stewart look-alike, but with the addition of sagging jowls, a pair of thick, black-rimmed glasses and an oxygen tube that snaked from his nose to a rolling tank. It was about a hundred degrees in his apartment and he was still wearing a wool plaid shirt. The boys stood there stunned as if they've never seen an old guy before.

"Damn," Bish sputtered. "Age sure does change a fella."

"And how," said StuBoy.

I reached over to shake Lefty's hand. Pen followed. "We found a box of Bish's photos and this envelope of negatives was in there with your name on them," I explained.

"We had prints made for you," Pen added.

Lefty took the pictures and sat back down. "Please, have a seat," he said, motioning for us to sit on the couch. "Now, how do you know my crew?"

"She's Smitty's granddaughter," blurted StuBoy, giving Lefty a big wink. Bish elbowed StuBoy in the ribs.

Lefty reached up to adjust his hearing aid.

"My grandma was engaged to Bish during the war," I explained. "But when he got killed, his buddy Smitty—Grandpa Chuck to me— brought his things to Merrilee, my grandma. Chuck and Merrilee wound up getting married. Chuck died a year or so ago and we've been cleaning out the house so Grams can move. We found a whole box of Bish's stuff in the hayloft of the horse barn. These were in there with your name on them. That's why we decided to try to find you."

I didn't mention that I'd seen him severely hung over in Bish's memory.

Lefty frowned and raised his chin as if he was examining Bish and the guys. Wild white eyebrows rose above his glasses. He shook his head and pawed the photo negatives out of the envelope with shaky hands. "Feinstein," he called out. "Here's one of you."

Lefty waved the photo of a young guy with dark curly hair. "Finney was the singing bombardier back in the day. He and Naussman been hanging around here for a while now, but don't tell the help. They'll think I've dropped off the deep end."

I scanned the room as two more bomber boys appeared on Poe's piano bench.

"About time you boys showed up." Feinstein tipped his hat to Bish, StuBoy and Valentine. Feinstein's round face, sweet dark eyes, and big smile made me like him right away.

"You can thank the girls," said Bish, eyeing me. "Sure is swell to see you two again."

Lefty's eyes flitted back and forth between the boys. "Am I seeing things, or has the rest of my crew finally reported for duty?"

I shrugged, trying not to freak him out. "Yep, they're here," I said. "One last mission."

Lefty seemed fine with all the visitors. Pen was the one who got tweaky.

"Where are they?" She whispered to me, uncrossing and recrossing her legs, looking around the room.

I pointed toward the piano. "Just say 'hi' and get over it."

Pen fluttered a nervous wave. "Hi, boys," she said.

"Howdy, gorgeous," said Feinstein, raising his eyebrows and giving her a nod.

"Hey, she's my gal," said StuBoy, heading for Feinstein.

Bish grabbed StuBoy's arm. "For crying out loud, calm down."

Lefty cleared his throat. "Good to see you boys. It's been way too long."

"Yes, sir. Reporting for duty, sir," said Valentine.

Lefty noticed that Penelope was looking everywhere but at the bomber boys. "They're right there, dear," he said, pointing to Bish and the boys. "Bish, StuBoy, Valentine—my tail gunner, engineer, and radio operator." He waved his hand toward the piano bench. "And there, my copilot Naussman and bombardier Feinstein." Poe patted Pen's hand. "You see them, dear?"

Pen wilted and shook her head. "Nope. Darn it. I try, but Sylvie's the one with the gift."

Lefty looked at me with questioning eyes.

I nodded. "I see and hear them. That's one of the reasons we came here—to find out if I'm crazy."

"You're probably the sanest one here," Lefty said, smiling. He pointed a shaky finger at StuBoy and Valentine. "Damn shame about you boys. I remember reading the reports. Couldn't believe we'd lost you just like that."

StuBoy waved him off. "Don't make no difference now."

Bish paced back and forth. "Whatcha doing in this place, Lefty?" he asked.

Lefty glanced at his knees then up at Bish. "The wife died a few years back. Kids said I shouldn't live on my own. Seems my mind is sharp as ever, but my body is kaput." He inhaled, sucking life from his oxygen tube.

"Lung troubles?" asked Pen.

Lefty spoke on the exhale. "Lung, prostate, ticker—you name it."

"How about you leave it all behind and come with us?" said Bish. "We've got one last mission to fly." Bish slid the tiny bomber out of his pocket and sent it flying around the room. Obviously, he'd been practicing.

Uncertainty splashed across Lefty's face, then melted it into a lopsided smile. "I've been dreaming of flying."

The gist of what the boys were saying worried me. "No, wait," I blurted. "The truth is, Bish is on a mission and we need your help." I passed the crew photo to Poe. "We need to know what really happened on this mission. It was a strafing run, right?"

Lefty actually cringed. "Strafes didn't count," he said, coughing into his handkerchief.

"At least not to the military—who was doing the counting." Co-pilot Naussman spoke for the first time. "We hated those runs.

Dropping bombs from 8,000 or 10,000 feet was one thing, but flying low and seeing the faces of people running for their lives was enough to haunt a fella for the rest of his life."

"You got that right," said Feinstein. "I was right down there in the nose."

"It did haunt Bish," I said, scooting my chair closer to Lefty. Bish leaned in to get a better look at the crew photo too. "It set him in a tail spin that wouldn't quit."

"I know," said Lefty. "That was one helluva day. I don't know what happened in the back except what I heard on the i-com and later in the interrogation room. This picture was taken at the start of the mission. If it'd been taken when we got back to base not a one of us would be smiling."

CHAPTER SIXTEEN

THE CREW PHOTO

Lefty's hand started to shake and the crew photo fluttered to the floor. Both Bish and I reached for it, and as we made contact, the photograph began to glow and shift from black-and-white to color, to 3-D. Naussman and Feinstein jostled around behind me, and I felt the metal runway plates digging into my knee. Propellers roared, and my mouth was gritty with Corsican dust.

"Load up!" shouts Lefty after the base photographer snaps our pic.

Valentine and I head for the plane's back hatch. Poe, Naussman, Feinstein, and StuBoy make for the front.

We're all business. StuBoy checks the engines. Valentine checks his radio. I check our guns. "Bomb load secure," says Feinstein, and in minutes Lefty and Naussman have us in the air, flying in formation above the Tyrrhenian Sea. I crawl back to my stool in the tail position and wave to Corsica, secretly praying we'll make it back alive. I like it back here in the tail now—best view in the house.

The ship skitters and bumps through the air currents that stir the sea below. We're nearly 8,000 feet above the water and the air is December cold. Somebody was thinking when they issued our fleece-lined coats and pants. Even still, cold air seeps through the canvas gun cover and around the anti-flak barrier. The metal gun handles are coated with frost.

"Everything clear back in the tail?" says Lefty as we get our oxygen masks and interphone mics into place.

"All clear. We could use a little heat back here, though," I say.

"Just think of your sweetheart," says Lefty. "That'll warm you right up. Valentine, how you doing? Waist guns ready?"

"Ready and waiting, sir," says Valentine.

"StuBoy, all ready in the turret?"

"Sure thing, boss," says StuBoy. "Let's clear some Krauts and get the hell home."

"Feinstein," says Poe. "How's our progress to the target?"

"Steady and ready," shouts Feinstein through the i-com. "We're about 100 miles out."

"Coming in over Pisa," says Naussman. "Watch for flak and fighters, boys. We're dodging the vermin by making a high beeline right over the city tops."

Flak explodes below us. The formation holds tight.

"Little buggers are feelin' feisty today," says Feinstein.

"I-com clear," says Poe. "We've got new orders. Seems the guys on the ground need a little backup. We're peeling off to hit Ala. There's a large supply dump near there. Feinstein, got our coordinates?"

"Yes, sir."

"We strafe first, then circle and drop," says Poe. "Got it?"

"10-4," we all chime.

One foot forward, one back, I brace myself and eye the three other ships that follow us out of formation. It's not a usual maneuver and the ship bounces. I fling one hand out to steady myself and keep one hand on the guns, riding the plane's buck like a bronc buster. Flak explodes on either side. "StuBoy, Valentine," I say, scanning the ground. "Tower at nine o'clock."

We swing our guns and fire, causing an explosion below.

"Bingo!" Valentine and I say in unison.

We fly on, meeting the Adige River and following the train tracks northward.

"Kraut infested rail station is the target," says Feinstein. "We're aiming for building and vehicle destruction, not civilians or houses."

"Nose and turret, you fire straight on. Waist, you cover on the sides. Tail, you clean up as we pull up," commands Lefty. "Got it?"

"Got it," we echo.

We're last in a line of four planes dropping in low over the small town. My muscles strain with watching our back. We're wide open for fighter attack, but there's nothing in sight. Lefty calls out a warning then dives down for the run. Front guns wail. I hear the boom of Feinstein's cannon.

"School at 9 o'clock. Watch your fire!" shouts Feinstein.

I see the destruction then. Smoking trucks, train cars blown to bits, a gaping hole in the side of the station. "Clean it up Bish; don't stop shooting till we're in the clear."

Months of training kick in. Guns hammer, shells clank and careen throughout the body of the bomber. People on land scatter like rats, running every which way in the confusion. Why don't they stay inside? I think, swinging my guns from left to right in a killer arc. The plane is low, so low it seems her belly might scrape the building tops. Lefty is good at this stuff, knows just how much to push his ship.

"Pulling up," calls Naussman.

Feet jam against the floor-mounted gun support, arms press against the gun grips so I don't do a header into the plexi-blister. As it is, I fall forward plenty, enough to lock eyes with a tiny girl hiding behind a truck next to a body. A woman. Crumpled and bloody. My guns fire at a train engine. It blows, but the little girl doesn't seem to notice. The gun keeps firing and I keep staring—willing the tiny girl to stay still, to take cover. I try to unlock my fingers from the gun trigger, but they've been trained to grip. When she finally does move, it's directly into my line of fire.

"No!" I yell.

Bullets pierce her tiny body, spinning her in mid-air before leaving her sprawled on the road, still and bloody as the woman she had been crouched over.

"Oh, god; oh, God; oh GOD," I howl, sounding like some sort of animal.

"Bish!" yells Lefty. "Are you hit?"

"Goddammit! I told her to stay down," I yell. "She was supposed to stay down."

"Valentine! What's going on back there?"

The waist gunner hadn't seen what I had seen. Too much of the plane obstructed his view. Too much had happened in too little time. Should I cover my hit?

"Can't say," says Valentine. "People started running every which way. I was doing my darndest to aim at trucks and cars."

"I hit a truck," says StuBoy. "And how."

"Bish?" says Lefty.

"I-I hit an engine," I say, my mouth dry, tears freezing.

"Hold it together boys," says Naussman. "We need you to

cover our tail. We still have a drop to make. Hold it together."

Feinstein begins to hum.

"Target in sight," says Naussman.

"Pardon me, boys," Feinstein hums one of his little ditties as he gets ready to drop. *"Is that the Kraut-sniffin' choo choo, ooo ooo?"*

"Bish, what do you see?" asks Lefty.

I shake myself and peer out the blister, wanting to see those bombs more than anything. But instead, all I see is a replay of the little girl looking at me, hair in braids, dark eyes full of fear and hate, tiny body spinning with the impact of the bullets. My stomach goes queasy with the smell of my own breath.

"Hit!" Valentine chimes in. Smoke billows from the supply dump the ships in front of us had already managed to damage. Flak splatters at us with renewed vengeance. Guns fire all around me. I don't know where to aim.

"Bish?" says Lefty over the interphone. "You still with us?"

I snap my goggles against my face. "Yeah, yeah, I'm here. Fine. Just dandy."

"Shittyschmitts at ten o'clock," says StuBoy. "Let's get 'em." StuBoy lets fly from the turret. I try to aim at the little German fighters that buzz through the sky, but all I see is that little girl's face.

"Bish, fire!" yells StuBoy. "They're in your range."

My shots go wild. I can barely see beyond the tears that flood my goggles.

"What the hell?" shouts Valentine. "Bish, are you blind?"

The Messerschmitts sashay behind us, aiming straight at me. Serves me right.

"Bish! Shoot those motherfuckers!" shouts Valentine.

Plexi cracks. A bullet whizzes by, tearing at my thigh. "I'm hit!" I yell. "Goddammit, I'm hit."

"Hang on, Bish," says Lefty. "Hang on."

It's strange. Instead of pain, I feel like I'm waking up. "I'm okay," I whisper to myself. My vision clears as I shove my goggles onto my forehead. "I'm okay," I say loud enough for the crew to hear.

My guns fire and the two Shittyschmitts spiral out of range, wings smoking.

Lefty and Naussman steer the ship back into formation, heading south over friendlier territory. My hands still clench the gun controls.

"Sing us home, Mr. Feinstein," says Lefty. "Maybe we'll all start breathing again."

"Fools rush in," Feinstein sings softly. *"Where angles fear to tread...."*

Sweat trickles down my spine and I shiver. Leastways I didn't pee myself like some boys do. I run my hand along my leg, searching for an injury. Nothing. It's strange. Judging from the looks of my plexi, I should be dead. Closing my eyes in thanks, I slide backwards off my stool and hug it. Loose ammo shells swill around my feet.

"Damage check," orders Naussman.

"Engines clear," reports StuBoy.

"No holes in the belly," says Valentine. "But it looks like we've got a couple nicks in the tail."

I try to focus on the damage reports, to not let the smell of gunpowder, grease, and exhaust get to me. But I can't get the filmstrip of the little girl to stop running through my head. Sliding over to a belly hatch, I tug it open, lift my mask, and puke.

"Bish?" It's Naussman. "Bish, how'd you fare back there?"

Valentine puts a hand on my back and passes me a rag.

"We've got a busted blister," reports Valentine as I wipe my face. "But we still have a tail gunner." Valentine grips my shoulder.

Not much of one, I think before passing out.

When I blinked back to reality, Bish was gone and I was left holding the crew photo. Lefty snoozed in his chair, breathing in time with the hiss of his oxygen tank.

"Syl, are you okay?" said Pen. "You kinda spaced there for a minute."

"Where is he? Where are they?" I whispered.

"You're asking me?" said Pen. "What happened?"

"Oh, geez." I rubbed a hand over my face. "Bish just showed me what this whole mission is about. Now I get why he has to make right. He killed a tiny little girl."

"He can do that? He can show you stuff?" Pen's eyes went about as big as the sunflowers on her shirt.

"Yeah, it happens sometimes when we're touching the same thing."

"What happens?"

"We tap his memories. I was with him, as him, when he shot her."

"Holy shit." Pen sat down next to me. "Can you do that with the other guys?" she asked.

I shook my head. "I don't think so. It only works with Bish." Truth is, I didn't want to. Bish's memories were freaky enough.

Lefty snorted himself awake, and coughed so hard it sounded like he'd crack in two. "Bish. Where's Bish?" he said, shaking himself awake.

"Right here sir," said Bish, stepping through the window. I did a double take at the little bomber plane that had grown to full-size on the green outside Lefty's window.

"It wasn't your fault, you know," said Lefty.

Bish squatted next to his old pilot, his one-time roommate. "You know, Lefty, I tried to tell myself that. Even thought I'd let it all go—stopped caring what people thought or whether I lived or died—but I've never been able to shake the feeling that every person in the room hates me as much as I hate myself for what I did."

"Bish, buddy," said Valentine. "We peeled off because we had intelligence that some Axis leaders were holed up in the rail station. We were following orders."

Lefty and all the other guys nodded. "Strafing was a rarity by that point in the war." Poe rolled out the words with care. "We called them Surprise Parties."

"There's nothing quite like having a front row seat at a scene of mass destruction." Feinstein toed the carpet, hands in pockets. "I never told anybody this, but when I had to go flat on my belly at the front gun at close range like that, I closed my eyes."

Bish rubbed his temple. "Jiminy crackers, I wish I'd done that. I've never been able to get that little girl out of my mind."

"Bish saw the worst of it, that's for sure." Lefty nodded. "But we all have to take the blame. 'Buildings and trucks, buildings and trucks.' That was my chant. But when people swarm out of a place like bees from a kicked hive, what do you do?"

"If she'd just stayed where she was," said Bish. "I told her to stay put. I told her. She had such angry, piercing eyes."

"It's no wonder you went a little crazy afterward," said Lefty.

"What did the docs call it? Something ridiculous like Functional Nervous Disorder. We called it Good Man's Guilt."

StuBoy turned to Bish, clenching his arm. "That little girl gave you the Evil Eye. I'll swear on my own grave she did. It explains everything. And that whole deal when you disappeared into the hills?"

"We all saw, and did, and heard about unbelievable things back then," cut in Naussman. "Not a one of use wants to believe we could have done any of them."

Valentine looked out the window at the ghostly plane. "What was that saying, boys? *C'est la guerre.* This is war."

"Chi fa," is more like it, said StuBoy. "What can we do?"

Pen took the crew photo from me. She studied it for a sec, then looked at Lefty. "So what you're saying is that when we go to Italy, and somehow miraculously find the family of this little girl, we need to ask forgiveness for all of you bomber boys?"

"Sure. That's right," said StuBoy.

"Damn straight," said Valentine.

Naussman squeezed Bish's shoulder. "We were all in that ship together."

Feinstein blinked his eyes and nodded.

"And in the darkest hour of our darkest night," Lefty the Poet rambled in response. "There is delivered from the light, two girls young and bold, nurses of our sad, singed souls." Lefty coughed and wheezed into his handkerchief. "Rumor has it you boys are here to pick me up."

Pen looked at me.

"Can't fly a plane without a pilot," said Naussman.

"But I have to die to fly?"

Valentine put his hand on Poe's shoulder. "That's how it works, sir."

Lefty took a deep, gravelly breath. "So it's an evening run?"

"That's right," said StuBoy.

"Wait a second. Hang on, everybody," I said. "This is all real touching, but nobody's going anywhere yet. Mr. Poe, we came here because we thought you might have some contacts that could help us track down the family of this little girl in Ala."

"We did?" whispered Pen. "I thought we were just delivering—"

I elbowed her and she stopped in mid sentence.

Lefty cracked a slow, tired smile. "My book. Just take my book. It's over there on the desk. I don't need it anymore. There was a fella in

Italy. Contacted me some time ago. A professor, I think." He closed his eyes, sucked hard on his oxygen. Clearly we'd traumatized the old boy.

I squeezed Lefty's cold hand, then moved to his desk to look for his address book. "It's leather," he managed to wheeze out. "Benedicci," he said after a long inhale. "That's the name."

The book was easy to find on the tidy desk. "Leonard Allyn Poe" was stamped in faded gold on the worn leather cover. Inside, every contact had been written in neat handwriting in alphabetical order. "Benedicci" was right there. "Napoleon Benedicci, Trento, Italy." After all the picking and sorting I'd done at Grams's house it seemed too easy, but who am I to question Luck?

"Thanks, Lefty," I said. "We might pull off this mission yet." As I picked up the book, I noticed a small torn note framed between two pieces of glass perched on the desk.

And yet the menace of the years,
Finds and shall find me unafraid.

It was Bish's handwriting. I'd swear. Again. It was just like the note I'd swiped from Grandpa Chuck's mirror and put in my journal.

"Where did you get this?" I held up the framed note and turned to Lefty. StuBoy put his finger over his lips and pointed to the sleeping poet.

"We all had a piece," whispered StuBoy. "Bish gave 'em to us."

"What is it?" asked Pen.

I held up the framed note so that Pen could see.

"It's the poem 'Invictus' by William Henley," said Bish. "Any fella worth a damn knew that poem. I copied it down before we all shipped out from the States, and tore it apart so each of us could keep a piece."

"Said it would always bring us boys back together," said Valentine, pulling his piece of the poem out of his address book. Naussman, Feinstein, and StuBoy all nodded, digging around in wallets and shirt pockets to produce their pieces.

"They all had a piece of the poem, Pen," I explained. "Bish told them it would keep them tight."

"I haven't looked at this since the day I died," said Valentine.

Feinstein smiled and read his note. "Out of the night that covers me, black as the pit from pole to pole...."

StuBoy picked up where Feinstein paused. "I thank whatever gods may be for my unconquerable soul."

"In the fell clutch of circumstance, I have not winced nor cried aloud," added Valentine. "Under the bludgeonings of chance, my head is bloody but unbowed."

As the boys continued, the clouds outside grew dark. Death hovered like a giant black octopus above the B-25 parked on the lawn.

Naussman plowed on anyway. "Beyond this place of wrath and tears looms the horror of the shade." He put his hand on Poe's shoulder and nodded at me.

"And yet the menace of the years finds and shall find me unafraid," I read from the framed note in my hand.

Poe opened his eyes and stared beyond his picture window as Death beckoned.

Bish added his part. "It matters not how strait the gate, how charged with punishments the scroll—." Sunlight broke through the heavy clouds. "I am the master of my fate; I am the captain of my soul."

The Poet's eyes fluttered. "Weather's clearing. Time to load up, boys," said a tired Leonard Allyn Poe. He smiled and settled back into his recliner.

Naussman gave the thumbs up. "Rendezvous at Maria Dolens, 2100 hours," he said to Bish, StuBoy, and Valentine. "And get there early, there's bound to be traffic."

Poe had gone slack in the chair, his eyes on the plane. "Oh, crap, tell me the dude's not dying," said Pen, feeling Poe's wrist. "We gotta get someone."

I reached for Pen's arm, watching Naussman and Feinstein help the old poet stand and head toward the window.

"He's okay," I said. "He's got his crew."

By the time all six guys reached the plane, Poe was young and agile again. He ran a loving hand along the side of the olive green B-25, then turned to salute Death, Bish, and the boys before disappearing through the front hatch.

CHAPTER SEVENTEEN

THE EIGHT BALL

"**A**re the bomber boys still with us?" said Pen when we got in the car. "They're not bailing, are they?"

"Nope," I said. "Our guys are coming with."

I eyed the boys in the backseat through the rearview mirror. "Cause we're stuck like glue to you." StuBoy laughed.

"That's what you get for calling us out," said Bish.

Air rumbled sarcastically from between my lips. "Flies on fly paper."

"Ouch," said Valentine.

"The other guys, Poe and his buds, are apparently meeting us in Italy in a ghost bomber." I glanced at Pen.

She smiled. "And that doesn't sound weird at all."

"Just roll with it," I said to Pen. To Bish, I said, "For the record, I didn't mean to call you out." I thought back to that drizzly afternoon by the burn pile when I'd wished like heck for my grandfather, thinking that, if anything, I'd get a sign from Grandpa Chuck. I flashed on the ooglie-boogling of StuBoy and Valentine's pictures. It was supposed to be a joke. Now I could hardly imagine life without them. "But since you're here, you all can go to the stinkin' foreclosure sale with me. Kate's gonna entertain Grams, and Mom has already decided I'm on reconnaissance."

FORECLOSURE SUCKS

They say they hold the auctions
On the courthouse steps.
That's bull. It's inside near
A vending machine and a
Beat-up square pillar.
The lawyer looked young,
Nervous that the granddaughter of an owner was there
To watch the proceedings

When Pen, the boys, and I got home, we found Grams on the floor of my room surrounded by the contents of Bish's box. "Oh, what I wouldn't give to be there with him," she said. The picture she was lost in was of Bish, posing above tiled rooftops, umbrella pines, a basilica dome. On her knee rested a green and gray pamphlet titled "A Soldier's Guide to Rome."

I was glad to see her smiling, and relieved to see she hadn't torched the box.

But one big question still ate at me. "Where are your letters, Grams?" I asked, thinking of the notes in Bish's diary—"One from mother, one from Hound Dog, three from Merrilee."

She looked at me bewildered; Bish answered in my ear. "They were buried with me. My last demand."

"There was something I meant to tell him," Grams said. "But he left before I could."

"It's not as if I left by choice," Bish grumbled. "Who knew I'd survive 59 missions only to die in a stupid accident. That damn dumb Tetro never cleared his guns."

"What do you say we blow this place and go find Bish?" I said to Grams.

She smiled at me and nodded. "That'd be nice."

"Don't worry," I whispered to Pen as I did a double check for Grams's and my passports and boarding passes. It was two days after the foreclosure sale, day 18 of Bish's mission (not that he was counting or anything), and we were standing at SeaTac's Gate N3 in line to board a flight to Amsterdam—three girls and three ghosts. I felt like a rock star with an entourage. "My mom won't even notice we're gone," I said to Pen. "For all she and Kate know, I'm staying with Grams at Grace for the next five days. And for anybody else, hey, lots of grandmothers take their granddaughters on European vacations." I put my arm around Grams and grinned.

"Right," said Pen, drawing out the middle of the word and nervously flipping the pages of her passport.

"Good thinking," said Bish. "Besides, Merrilee and her best pal were about your same age when she took the train all the way to Virginia to see me off."

The herd moved forward. The bomber boys walked up and down the line of people as if they were doing an inspection. StuBoy tapped the businessman in front of us on the shoulder. "Hey pal, save me a seat, will ya?" The businessman rubbed his ear and tweaked his shoulder before handing his ticket to the attendant.

I laughed, and Grams turned to me. "What's so funny?"

"Nothing. I'm just so excited. Were you this excited when you went to see Bish in Virginia?"

Grams looked puzzled.

"That's so romantic," said Pen. "Traveling all the way across the country to wish your sweetie a safe good-bye."

"Wasn't that the last time you saw him?" I said, trying to prompt her. "Before he shipped out to Italy?"

"Oh yes, that was quite a trip."

I handed our tickets to the airline agent and felt bad that Grams was trying to cover for her blank memories. God, it must be such a drag to know you have file cabinets of memories inside your head but no keys.

"You're in seats 27 A, B, and C. Enjoy your flight." The airline agent tilted his head and flashed super white teeth. They went with his wiry bod and perfectly mussed hair.

"Thank you," said Grams, smiling. "We sure will."

"You have the best hair," said Pen to the agent as she took her ticket and followed us down the boarding bridge.

I turned off my phone with a sweaty touch and heaved a sigh of relief. First gatekeeper passed. My spinning stomach slowed a notch.

"What kind of a stewardess is that?" said Bish to StuBoy and Valentine.

StuBoy tapped the plastic of the plane interior when we got stopped up at the doorway. "What kind of ship is this? Plastic would never hold up under attack."

It occurred to me that these guys had never even seen a modern airplane. As we eased down the plane aisle, Valentine whistled at the seats. "Damn site plushier than that old bucket of bolts we sailed across on."

"That was some crossing, and how," said Bish. "Hurricanes, U-boats."

The three of them went silent and disappeared into the back of the plane. It must have been weird for them to be going back to the place they died. My mind wandered off to Bummerland. How did they die? What happened? Where were they buried? It was the first time I'd really thought about them actually being, you know, dead-dead. They joked about it, but the reality was only just now sinking in. Truth was, I didn't think of them as dead guys anymore. It was more like they were stuck in another dimension.

Once we were in the air, Grams and Pen slipped into snooze mode. I took my journal and the travel album of Bish's photos I'd made and moved into a nearby empty row. The picture of two planes flying in formation above a volcano caught my eye, and I started to sketch.

"Oh, damn," said Bish, appearing in the seat next to me. "Hey boys, she pulled *The Eight Ball*."

I looked for something on the planes in the picture that was *Eight Ball*-ish. Other planes had painted noses, like *Miss Fancy Pants* with the Hooter's chick or *Shit House Mouse* with its outhouse. This one had nothing but a bunch of numbers—and patches.

"Add a couple of bullet holes there," said StuBoy, pointing to the plane's tail as he and Valentine materialized to my left.

"And a busted wing-tip there," said Valentine, "and you have our little death trap."

"*Death Trap*? Awesome name for a plane," I said.

"Not if you're in it," said Bish.

My breath caught with the realization that this plane had been the death of them. "You guys died in this plane, didn't you?"

The boys glanced from one to another.

"Not in it," said Bish.

"And not all of us," said Valentine. "By the way, you need some flames coming out of that engine, there." He pointed to the engine on the plane's right wing. "Now show us jumping out with parachutes, and you about have it."

"You mean you got out? I thought your plane was shot down or it exploded or something."

"Oh, hell, we'd still be alive if it weren't for that damn band of Blackies," said Valentine.

StuBoy nodded. "And how."

I slid the photograph of *The Eight Ball* out of the album sleeve. "Show me," I said, holding the photo out to Bish.

He shook his head as StuBoy and Valentine nodded, slow and strong.

"Show her," said Valentine firmly. "Maybe for once our lives can be more than a damn two-liner."

My eyes slid to Bish.

"Ah, heck, Sylvie. You don't want to see that," he said. "None of us want to revisit that day."

Valentine frowned. "Maybe we don't want to, but we do."

StuBoy nodded. "He's right. We can't stop revisiting that day. That's what happens when a fella never gets the chance to debrief. Used to be we'd come back to the interrogation room after a mission, recount what went on, and move on."

Valentine nodded, a weary mournfulness I'd never seen before in his eyes.

"Then tell me what happened," I said. "Consider it your official debrief." Closing my journal, I put the photo on the flip-down tray and opened Bish's diary. I placed my hand on an incomplete April 13 entry. "Bish, it's time to finish this one."

StuBoy adjusted his cap. "She's right. Fleming, our pilot *du jour* only had part of the story when he made his report. Good guy, but pilots tend to only see what's in their windscreen."

"Go on, Bish ol' buddy," said Valentine. "You know I'd do it if I could." Valentine reached out to touch the diary, but Bish moved like lightning. He not only touched the diary, he put his hand on top of mine.

Bish and I had never touched before, and it was cold at first. Then, as our hands merged to rest on the page, my fingers began to tingle and warmth spread through my hand. Bish nodded at Valentine and StuBoy, and they both reached over and added a hand to the pile. Their energy rushed through me, catching me in a raging river that swept me back into Bish's 1945.

My stomach bunches as I lie on my bunk and begin an entry in my diary. Now that so many of our office personnel have been shipped home, I'm glad I picked up this diary in Roma. Like Poe, I've taken to noting my missions and targets here, but today there's bigger news to report.

13 APRILE–April; VENERDI–Friday

On standby for 49th mission. News came this morning that President Roosevelt died yesterday. It doesn't seem real. We have a mission anyway, and the boys are ready as ever to finish this thing and go home. But how will we win this war without old FDR? Got mail from Smitty. No letters from Merrilee going on four days now. She needs a scolding—

"Bishop, briefing time. On the double," shouts Tactical Officer Folsom.

I stow my diary in my locker and leap off the bunk. StuBoy and Valentine hustle on ahead of me. We already have our crew assignments when we go into briefing and aren't the first group to say their prayers when assigned to *The Eight Ball.*

Folsom removes his hat once we've gathered, and the rest of us boys follow suit. "A moment of silence for President Roosevelt, God rest his soul," says Folsom.

I close my eyes and hear the inhale and exhale of airmen, the uneasy scuffle of boots on dirt flooring. My hat feels heavy in my hands. Why hasn't Merrilee written? I know I should be paying respects to Roosevelt, but I can't stop worrying about Merrilee.

"In the words of our late, great President," says Folsom. "'More than an end to war, we want an end to the beginning of all wars—yes, an end to this brutal, inhuman and thoroughly impractical method of settling the differences between governments.'"

We've all seen the brutality, the inhumane treatment of prisoners everywhere, know firsthand about the impracticalities of this long war. The ache to go home, to see Merrilee, rattles through me. I want to put what had started out as pure and naive patriotic duty behind me. Damn the terms of enlistment—duration of the war plus six months.

"Remember, gentlemen," Folsom's voice cuts through my thoughts. "That's why we're here." I clench my teeth and wipe a renegade tear from my eye. "We're running frontline support today," Folsom says. "We know there's a Kraut command station at the northern tip of Lake Garda." Folsom circles the town of Arco on the wall map. "We need every one of you to be on extra alert. There's sure to be plenty of flak and fighters between there and Rovereto, so buckle up boys, this ain't no milk run."

Dark circles show under most boys' eyes. The Krauts are fighting like cornered cats.

"To add to the possible complications," Folsom continues. "We've had rumors that the Black Brigade has been intercepting Allied supply drops. They're looking for 'chutes and they are not known for taking prisoners. My point? And this is for you, pilots. If you're hit, do whatever you can to get your plane back into Allied territory before anyone jumps. I pray that won't be necessary, but I warn you just in case."

I glance at StuBoy and Valentine as we file out of the briefing tent and into the trucks and jeeps that ferry us to the ships. Poe, Naussman, and Feinstein are flying lead anti-flak. Damn. Wish I were assigned to them. Instead StuBoy, Valentine and I are assigned to fly with Captain Fleming in the no-name jobber we'd nicknamed *The Eight Ball* because it comes back nicked and holed from nearly every mission. It's a work of art in patch metal.

We pile in and everything goes smooth as silk from take-off at Falconara Field to Ala. The day is clear and bright. From my tail blister, I can see the whole formation, fifteen other bombers fanned out in the usual four-by-four formation, with fighters at our flanks. I salute Poe and Naussman in a nearby ship. "This one's for FDR," I say, but my words are lost in the rumble of the engines.

Down below, Lake Garda sprawls to our left like a giant lazy teardrop, while the Adige River slithers along the mountains' skirts.

"Okay boys, quiz time," says Valentine into the i-com. "Who will be our next commander in chief, God rest our dear president's soul?"

Hicks, Fleming's new baby-boy copilot, chimes in. "Eleanor! She's one tough dame."

"I meant by the rules of the Constitution, not popular vote," says Valentine with a laugh.

"Oh, come on, numb nuts, it's Truman. VP Truman," I say.

"That's what I was gonna say," says McNeary. He's parked on his jump seat near the bomb bay. McNeary is a dead aim and earned his nickname "Eagle Eye" for good reason.

"Think he can end the war?" says Valentine, egging the boys on.

"I dunno if he can," says McNeary. "But me and my lads plan to nail every Kraut hole we see."

Valentine laughs. "You're the only guy I know who calls his bombs 'lads' as if they have a heart and soul."

"Well, I dunno about a heart and soul, but they sure as hell have minds of their own." McNeary clears his throat. "You gotta make 'em feel as if they're part of the team; otherwise they'll never hit their mark."

"And in case you didn't know it," says StuBoy, quoting McNeary, "dropping bombs is our business. It's why we're here, boys. Strategical Daylight Bombing. Ain't that right, Eagle Eye?"

McNeary laughs. "Sure enough."

"Well, you can be as 'strategical' as you want up there at the front of the plane, but back here it's all about keeping the damn Krauts off our tail," I say.

"Can it, boys," cuts in Fleming. "Target B in sight. And they've spotted us."

In a second, I've unlocked my guns.

"Let's knock us out some flak towers," says StuBoy.

"Yes indeedy," says Valentine.

"On it," I add.

I-com chatter stops, and even though Valentine, StuBoy, and I might wish we had Poe and Naussman up front, we've been in the game long enough to shrug it off and flip into fight mode. Flak explodes everywhere. We expected flak from Rovereto. Now anti-aircraft guns hammer from the hilltop at Arco too. Behind us, the formation splits in half. Fleming veers *The Eight Ball* east to hit Rovereto, while up ahead, *Miss Fancy Pants* and seven other planes speed north to the front.

Flak explodes in great black poofs, shaking the plane to its rivets. Fleming holds *The Eight Ball* steady. I aim at the flak towers below, combining fire with Valentine to take out one gun.

"Bingo!" we yell in unison.

"Primary target in sight!" shouts McNeary. It's a communication station and rail yard near the river.

The bomb bay clanks open, and McNeary dominates the i-com again. "In 5-4-3-2-1. Bombs-away!"

I'm too busy covering *The Eight Ball's* back end to watch the big old bomb StuBoy and I had decorated as an Easter Egg fall through the sky. Instead I spot the clouds of dirt rising from where the bombs crash through the sidewall and roof of the Axis Communications Station. The ships behind us drop their bomb loads too, some hitting the Communications Station, others popping rails and taking out supply cars along the Brenner Pass line.

"Hot damn! You can mark that drop 100 percent," I shout.

We're rejoicing in McNeary's strike when a set of fighters appears, guns blasting. Damn Krauts.

"Gimme my controls!" demands Fleming. The whole ship shimmies as the flight control lever sticks, then finally engages.

"Top Drawer's taking a beating at the fringe," says co-pilot Hicks. "And now they're firing at our Spam Can, the bastards."

"Pull up your plates, Bish!" StuBoy yells.

"Done!" I fire at one of the fighters. "Take that you little ball-licker," I shout, immediately following with a quick, muttered prayer. Is God really out here? If he is, I think as

I lay on my guns, I hope he's on our side. Ammo shells clutter the floor, swilling back and forth as the ship banks and turns, dodges and shimmies. A Messerschmitt dives at us, hammering at the engines.

"Dropping to evade," Fleming shouts into the i-com.

"Where are our fighters when we need them?" says McNeary, leaning on his guns.

The turret gunner in the plane behind us locks in on the Kraut fighter and begins firing.

Flak explodes to our left.

"Oh, sweet Jesus!" McNeary yells. "Bastard about got me."

"Are you hit?" shouts Fleming.

"I'm okay. I'm okay," McNeary yammers. "Motherfucker just got a little too close. Where is that guy? I'm gonna blast his balls off."

"He just got hit. One down," I say.

"Get us the hell outta here, Fleming, will ya?" McNeary shouts. "Mission accomplished."

"It was a setup," says Fleming. "Flak guns to the west, pushed us into guns and 'schmitts in the east. I'm doing my best to swing wide."

"Starboard engine on fire!" yells Valentine. "Engine on fire!"

"Hold on boys, we're gonna dive," says Fleming.

"The mountains are too close," yells Valentine.

Fleming banks instead, trying to blow out the flames. Ammo shells swill around our ankles again, a writhing catch of metal sardines captive in the back of the plane. *The Eight Ball's* very skeleton seems to shiver. "Don't worry, boys. This baby has pulled through worse," shouts Fleming. "She'll get us home."

The smell of burning oil fills the cabin. "Mother Mary of the Pronunciation, please deliver us from all evil." McNeary mumbles into the i-com. For a Catholic boy, he sure does foul up his saints.

My eyes are glued on the flames. "God damn it, Fleming. It's not working!"

"I've gotta kill the engines," he shouts back.

Flak explodes just above McNeary's turret. "Dive!"

McNeary shouts. Chunks of metal bite at our blisters. Fleming presses the plane downward into a valley.

"Say your prayers, boys," says Fleming. "I'm cutting the engines. We'll bring 'em back one at a time."

"Dear God, I'm sorry I led so many girls astray," says Valentine. "I promise if we get through this I'll mend my ways."

I can't help snorting. "And I'll make sure he keeps his promise." My mind goes to the little girl from Ala, a hill or two away, to the *lamella* I made for her. I should have thought to drop it as we flew over. Nothing will ever be right until that's delivered. "Please let me return safely to Merrilee," I whisper.

Fleming's shout shatters my concentration. "We're cutting in 5-4-3-2-1."

When the engines shut down, it's as if the whole world is holding its breath. Everything is quiet, just the sound of wind rushing past the ship. Fleming keeps the bomber on an updraft, us boys press our faces to the plex, watching and willing the fire to die. None of us dares to speak. Death's breath rattles the hatches, its fingers searching for an opening.

"Fire's out!" shouts Valentine.

"Pull up, Fleming," I shout. "Or we'll be wiping our asses with pine needles quicker than you can say Jackrabbit."

"Calm down back there," says Fleming. "Engines clear."

The ship shakes as propellers spin to a blur. *The Eight Ball* hums and rattles back to life.

"We're alive at five," says Fleming. He quickly noses the plane upward to clear a ridge and rejoins the scattered formation. But as he does, anti-aircraft guns hidden on the ridge above Rovereto flare into action. Flak rips a hole in *The Eight Ball's* belly.

"God damn Fascists!" says Valentine, yelling and shooting like a madman.

"Anyone hit?" Fleming asks over the i-com.

"No sir, but we've got a gaper on the port side," reports StuBoy. "About two-feet wide." Ammo casings jiggle and spill from *The Eight Ball's* wound. Valentine's maps flap and crackle.

"More flak at eleven o'clock!" Bish shouts. Too late for Fleming to dodge, *The Eight Ball's* left wing tip is torn clean off and our one good engine flares.

"Damn it!" says Fleming. For the first time, I hear fear in his voice.

"Stay steady, boys," says copilot Hicks. "We're still in the game."

I check my chute.

The plane jolts. "Just get us to some neutral ground," says McNeary.

"Mac, boys, you need to get the hell out." Fleming's voice is frantic. "I'm gonna try to set her down in the river valley, but there's a good chance we won't make it. Release all hatches."

The plane veers dangerously near to one of the other bombers in the formation as *The Eight Ball's* engines sputter and die.

"I'm riding her out as long as I can to make a diversion," shouts Fleming. "You boys jump!"

Metal screeches as *The Eight Ball* cracks.

"Bomb bay open. I'm out!" says McNeary. I see him falling below and back as we sail southward over him.

I scramble out of the tail to meet up with StuBoy and Valentine. We unlatch the back hatch, and I motion for StuBoy to go. It's too noisy to talk now that we're unplugged from the i-com, so StuBoy and I give each other the thumbs up and I thump him on the back before he slips through the hatch.

I motion to Valentine to go next, but the damn fool shakes his head. The plane lurches and skids through the air, knocking us to our knees. I push Valentine toward the hatch and he dives head first through the hole in the plane's tail only to get a leg tangled in the hatch ladder. He's hanging upside down as showers of flak rain around us. Murphy and his "laws" may be Death's friend and *The Eight Ball* his play toy, but not us, not now. Dropping to my belly, I slide out of the hatch and wrench Valentine's foot free. He flops away like the rag doll my sister once threw from the rafters of our barn. "Pull," I yell. "Don't forget to pull."

A second later, I'm somersaulting after Valentine. The ground seems far, far away, but I'm falling fast. I tug at my ripcord, and once I'm floating, I see two other silk 'chutes soaring through the flak-torn sky.

Miles away, I see *The Eight Ball* plow belly-first into an

open field. There's no explosion, and I hope Fleming and Hicks are okay.

It's a known fact that us boys have a better chance of survival in numbers. We each carry a safety kit and a revolver, although I've never known anyone who ever had to use them. I drift toward Valentine, both of us aiming for the same field where McNeary and StuBoy landed. The air currents pull me farther south, although my gut tells me it's not far enough. We're still headed for the fields and marshes south of Rovereto, still in enemy-occupied territory.

Below me, Valentine makes for a landing, but crumples and rolls end over end into a tangle of parachute lines. Trouble. Big trouble. I land a good mile away and, after gathering my chute and stowing it in a thicket, set out to find him.

I hear StuBoy's voice before I see him.

"Valentine! Valentine, buddy, you okay?" There's no answer.

When I make it over the small rise, I spot StuBoy, knife drawn, cutting Valentine out of the parachute that had wrapped around him like a shroud.

Three heads emerge behind StuBoy and I catch myself wondering how Fleming and Hicks had managed to make it here so fast. Two blinks later and I realize what an ass I am.

It's a weaponless McNeary being marched by a pair of Blackies at his back. StuBoy is caught unaware. Even from where I'm crouched in the tall grass, the finger-drawn flare-paint letters McNeary has painted on his chest are plenty obvious.

R-U-N.

Every ounce of me wants to, but I can't abandon my pals.

The death head insignias on the berets of the Black Brigade stand out in the afternoon sun. The Blackies carry a couple of old M91s. I aim at the leader, but he's way beyond my handgun range.

StuBoy glances at McNeary. "Help me make a splint," he says, seeming to not notice the Blackies.

A scruffy man dressed in black like his buddies rises out of the tall grass to StuBoy's left. His red armband is faded, but the Kraut-lover's swastika is plenty clear.

I crawl closer, staying under cover in the tall grass.

Scruffy speaks in quick Italian, waving four fingers.

Damn. He knows one of us is missing—four chutes, they saw four chutes.

Valentine, the best Italian speaker among us, pushes away the tangle of parachute lines, shakes his head, and runs a finger across his throat. *"Morto, finito,"* he says.

Scruffy frowns and shouts at the other two. They strip StuBoy and Valentine of their weapons and poke at them with their rifles to set them marching.

"Avanti," shouts Scruffy. *"Gehen!"*

StuBoy and McNeary help Valentine stand and take a few small steps, then a few more. The going is slow and obviously painful for Valentine. Scruffy scowls, walks up behind Valentine and shoots him through the chest.

"No!" yells StuBoy as Valentine slumps and falls to the ground. StuBoy spins and leaps at Scruffy. McNeary strikes the Blackie nearest him. Knee to gut. Left hook to jaw.

Gut churning, I take my cue and run like hell toward the bunch of them, blasting the one unoccupied Blackie before diving back into the grass. The young Italian in black is a goner before his *amicos* even know what's happening.

More shots cut through the air. I roll to my feet to take another shot. StuBoy's down, and Scruffy's taking aim at McNeary. Without a second's hesitation, I aim for Scruffy and shoot. Back under cover, I see the last Blackie turn to his writhing leader in surprise.

At that moment, McNeary takes his own advice and runs. I make to cover him, but before I can blast the little Blackie bastard to bits, McNeary goes down. I keep firing—for StuBoy, for Valentine, for McNeary—and put a bullet straight through the Kraut-lover's heart.

It's not until I move in to check my boys that I realize I've been hit in the thigh. Blood gushes from a deep graze. First taking the guns off the downed Blackies, I pick up StuBoy's knife and quick cut myself a black sleeve to use as a bandage. What the hell just happened? StuBoy, McNeary, and Valentine can't be dead. Hand to neck, I check for StuBoy's pulse. Nothing. Scruffy's dead eyes stare at me, and I shoot him again for good measure.

My heart thumps, and even though I want to see my pals cared for, orders ingrained in my brain push me away. I'm more good to them alive than dead. I reach down to close Valentine's eyes.

"Bish." Valentine's lips move, eyes slide half-way open. "Take...my...book."

My hand snaps back in surprise. Valentine's voice sputters. Blood spills from between his ribs. "Oh, buddy. Hang on," I say. "I'll get help."

Valentine tries to lift his hand, but it flops back to the ground after rising less than an inch. "Take my book," he says again.

Reaching inside Valentine's fleece-lined bomber jacket, I remove a tiny leather-bound address book from his shirt pocket.

"So many girls," Valentine wheezes. "So little time."

My vision blurs. I try to laugh but can't manage it. Death slides closer, arms reaching, lips searching for Valentine's wounds. I beat at it with the butt of my pistol.

"Write to them," Valentine breathes. "Tell them I'll never forget."

"No!" I say. "You hang on. Those girls want to hear from you, not me."

A smile tugs at Valentine's lips. "I gotta go. Ol' StuBoy's waiting."

I glance up, part of me half expecting to see StuBoy's ghost. But nothing—no one—is there. When I turn back to Valentine, he's still. Gone. I pound a shaking fist against the swastika still attached to the sleeve tied around my thigh. Pain screams through my leg and the horizon begins to sway.

CHAPTER EIGHTEEN

CHOICES

"All passengers please return to your seats." A woman's voice crackled through the plane's speaker system, jolting Bish, the boys, and me back to the present. The picture of *The Eight Ball* was at my feet, and Bish's diary had fallen between my leg and the side of the seat. I was reaching for the picture when the speaker blared again.

"Due to some unexpected turbulence, the captain has turned on the fasten seat belt sign."

StuBoy lifted the picture for me and I snatched at it before any of the other passengers could see the photo floating in midair. The plane bounced, but it was nothing like *The Eight Ball* fighting for its life. The bomber boys seemed unconcerned. Pen and Grams popped open their eyes.

"You're okay," I said from across the aisle. "No drinks to spill." The turbulence calmed and they closed their eyes again.

"Nothing like having your whole life go down in a two liner," said Valentine.

"You got that right," Bish said. "When I finally made it back to base, the report I saw said plain and simple, 'The 445th lost one ship above Rovereto. Four chutes seen: McNeary, Johnson, Valentine, and Bishop reported missing in action.'"

"But how did you get back to base?" I doodled a picture of a parachute. "What about the pilots, Fleming and Hicks?"

"They got back eventually," Bish explained. "Found a foxhole in a farmhouse. I hoofed it to the river and jumped a train going south. Hoped like hell our boys didn't bomb it on my way downriver." He rubbed his right thigh as if the pain still lingered. "Back at base, Fleming reported that he'd seen the Blackies attack. Updated the report to say, 'McNeary, Valentine, Johnson, and Bishop killed in action.' Sure did surprise the hell outta him when I showed up. You can bet your bombshells that I set that report straight. Thing that really fired me up was that the fool armorer on base who blew his own gut open got more of a memorial than our combat crew. Not that the kid didn't deserve it. It's just that most folks on base didn't want to know us crewmen because they figured we were already a bunch of goners. No mourning required."

"That's so wrong." I sketched Death the way I saw him—an ominous octopus whose tentacles sought out anyone anywhere.

StuBoy stared out the window like a zombie.

"What's bugging you, StuBoy?" I asked.

StuBoy shook his head. "I don't know, Syl. For me, dying isn't the worst of it. It was breaking a promise to my kid brother."

Valentine swatted the visor of StuBoy's cap. "You're not getting all sappy on us now, are you?"

StuBoy ignored him. "We were about to leave on a fishing trip when I got called up. Before I left, he made me promise I'd come back home to take him fishing. And if it hadn't been for that stinking band of Blackies, I'd have made it."

"Maybe," Bish said. "None of us knew how we were gonna go. Those promises we made to go fishing or get married were just ways of trying to tilt the odds. But it was all in our heads."

Valentine snorted. "Hell, now I feel shallower than a fry pan. All I ever regretted was never having a chance to be naked for a whole day with a beautiful woman."

The boys laughed. I rolled my eyes. "But I still don't get how you all are here," I said. "And why all you guys and not my Grandpa Chuck?"

StuBoy adjusted his hat. Valentine nodded at Bish. "This one's yours, old buddy."

"It's complicated, Sylvie," said Bish. "Death's options aren't the same for all of us." He took off his cap and twisted it in his hands, glanced at Grams, then at StuBoy and Valentine. "Boys who die in honorable action like these two can choose between permanent rest leave or helping out their buddies. Fellas who die of natural causes like Smitty, or Grandpa Chuck to you, get a choice between moving on with their memories intact or taking a swig of Lethe Lightning and forgetting everything. No regrets.

"Boys like me, who die in an accident—because some dang fool didn't discharge the ammo from his guns—get a different choice: Tackle your unfinished business via Final Mission or give it another go—as in reincarnate. I think you can figure out what choices we all made."

"And here I thought that when you died, that was it." I shrugged and bit my pencil.

"Oh no, darlin'," said Valentine. "Death doesn't make it that easy. It likes to play with its food."

CHAPTER NINETEEN

FINDING VENITIA

Once we arrived in Milan, Grams amazed me by flirting her way through getting a rental car. I figured the rental process would be dicey, but she just smiled and handed over her driver's license and credit card. "I'm here to find the lost love of my life," she told the twenty-something Adonis at the rental car counter.

"And the girls here agreed to help me." Grams reached for Pen and me.

Never mind that he's dead, I thought.

"He's right there," said StuBoy, standing on the rental car counter and pointing at Bish like he'd just finished a show tune.

"For crying out loud," said Bish. "You're supposed to be helping."

StuBoy threw up his hands and jumped off the counter.

"It's the most romantic story," Pen explained to the rental car guy. She was clearly working on adding an Italian boyfriend to her repertoire.

"You need map?" said the guy, winking at me. His brass name tag said Angelo.

"Thanks, but I Googled it all," I said, holding up a folder of map print-outs and suddenly feeling like a dork.

"Ah, but the Google, it can't know everything," he said, frowning. A lock of sun-bleached brown hair fell over one of his dark chocolate eyes.

"That's what I keep telling her," said Grams. She batted her big blues at him and signed the rental agreement.

"Me too," said Pen, pressing her double-Ds against the counter.

"We're going to Lake Guarda," I said. "Any chance you know anyone in Ala or Rovereto? We need to find someone who was alive during the war. World War II."

The guy shook his head, then brightened up. "*Si*, yes. I want to tell you go to Museo della Guerra. Scott, my American school friend, is guide there. In Rovereto." Angelo smiled. "I call him and tell him you coming, yes?"

"Uh—sure," I said, grabbing the handle of my wheelie bag.

Pen thumbed through the English–Italian phrase book we'd swiped from Bish's box. *"Si, grazie,"* she said, beaming.

Angelo laughed. *"Voi siete grande velocita."*

"We're staying at that nice big hotel," said Grams. "Sylvie, show him the picture."

"Hotel Davina?" Angelo asked.

"Yes. That's it," I said, hoping I hadn't just hooked us up with a serial killer.

The next morning there was a message for us at the hotel. Angelo had called to say that his buddy Scott suggested we look up anyone from the Pizziani family in Ala. Otherwise, he knew a number of people whose families had lived in the Rovereto area during World War II. They were docents at his museum and they love to talk— in Italian. I thought of StuBoy and Valentine's Black Brigadiers from Rovereto and decided it was a last-ditch option.

Lefty Poe's address book was in my backpack. I'd worked his professor angle by sending an email from the library just before leaving the States. I needed to find out if the professor had emailed back. As it turned out, Lefty was in some 57th Bomb Wing history group and those guys were super game to help. What was it about trying to find a dead guy? Even old Pietro at the hotel concierge desk had been eager to hear Bish's story when I showed him my little book of Bish's photos.

Leaving Pen and Grams by the pool, I went inside to check my email. The bomber boys trailed along.

I waved to Pietro as the boys and I settled at the bank of Internet computers. The professor had replied. Just the fact that he'd written back made my heart beat faster. He gave me four names from an oral history project featuring people who had lived in Ala during the war. One of them was Pizziani.

With Bish's phrase book in hand, I returned to old Pietro. *"Avete voi telephone—?"* I stumbled over the Italian words. "Sorry. Do you have a telephone book?" I asked Pietro, holding up the phrase book as an example.

"Si. You are looking for something I can help with?" he said.

I explained that I first needed to find a church with a deep well or pit—and possibly the family of a little girl who was killed during the war. "I have some names," I said, showing him my list and the photo book. "But I only have one more day."

Pietro put on his reading glasses and looked at the list and the pictures. "And-ah this is important, why?"

I fingered the little pouch that hung around my neck. The replacement *lamella* I made for Bish was inside. "We have to find a church—*chiesa*—in Ala," I said, folding my hands as if to pray. "So I can deliver a prayer."

Pietro frowned. "For what do you pray?"

"That's kinda private," I said.

"Si. Mi scuzi," said Pietro, closing the photo book and handing it back.

"My grandpa," I blurted, showing him Bish's picture. "At least I think he's my grandfather. He was here during the war."

"Grandpa?" said Bish, making a psht sound. "Unproven."

I wanted to smack him. Could he seriously think Grams slept with any one else while she was engaged to him?

Pietro pursed his lips and raised one bushy gray eyebrow as he looked at the picture. It was Bish's 50th mission photo, taken when he'd been stationed on Corsica. I flipped the page of my little photo book and showed him first a picture of Bish in Roma, then one of Bish on the beach.

"Ah, Capri," said Pietro. "This girl your grandmother?" He pointed at a brunette in the photo with Bish.

"No," I said. "I don't know who she is."

Pietro shook his head and made a tisking sound.

"Ah heck, she was nobody," said Bish. "Just some two-faced dame we met on the ferry."

"Your grandpapa, he is still alive?" asked Pietro.

I shook my head. Frowned. Did my best to look sad and pathetic.

"He died here?" asked Pietro. "In war?"

Nodding, I used my one chance. "His dying wish was that we come here to Ala to deliver a message."

"To a churcha?" Pietro's mustached lips let the question dangle.

"To the family of a little girl." I couldn't quite bring myself to say that he had killed her. "It's complicated. We came all the way from America to deliver a message to someone in Ala."

"I am trying to understand," said Pietro. "Does this someone have a name?"

"No doubt," I said, grinning. "I just have no idea what it is."

Pietro looked over the top of his glasses. "Then how will you deliver the message?"

I hopped from one foot to the other. "Well, all I really have to do is take a message to the chapel, the church there. I thought that if I could, I'd ask around to find the family. The town can't be that big. Plus, I have those names."

Wrinkles laced Pietro's forehead.

"Offer him a few bills," Bish said in my ear.

"Can you help?" I said.

Pietro fingered his mustache. "Maybe yes. Maybe no. I try."

"We're going to Ala first thing tomorrow morning."

Pietro nodded his head. *"Si, si.* Of course."

Back in the elevator, I fidgeted and couldn't help biting my lip.

"What's eating at you, Syl?" said Bish.

"Everyone is so nice, so helpful," I said. "It's almost too easy."

"That's how most folks were during the war," said StuBoy. "Remember all those little washer women at Falconara? Never seen anybody so eager to do my laundry."

"Their families were starving," said Valentine. "Stinkin' Krauts had bled them dry."

"Why do you always have to be such a damp rag?" said StuBoy.

"Somebody has to keep your boots in the bunker." Valentine sighed like he was tired of the job.

Bish looked at his watch. "Well, it ain't over till it's over," he said. "We're down to twenty-one hours, and I'll be damned if we're any closer to finding the drop spot than we were back in the States."

The elevator dinged and the doors opened on our floor. "That's crap," I said. "We're here, aren't we? In Italy. And at least we have some contacts. That's about 10,000 miles closer than we were back home. I put my butt on the line for you guys, and the least you can do is show a little thanks. You might get to go party it up when this is all over, but me? I already know I'm grounded for life."

A lady stepped out of her room and looked around, no doubt wondering who I was talking to. I held up my phone and she smiled.

The bomber boys faded a little and floated down the hall. "You told her about Maria Dolens?" I heard StuBoy ask Bish.

"Sure," said Bish.

"Well you better remind her, and on the double," said StuBoy. "We don't get to the Maria Dolens, we don't get home."

Early the next morning Pen, Grams, and I were walking through the lobby to get our car when Pietro waved at us. *"Buongourno,"* he said. "I find someone for you. My wife's mother's cousin is in Ala. She is silk trader, from a long family of silk traders. Ala is famous for the silk. They have the trees for the worms."

"That's great," I said. "How do we reach her? What's her name?"

He smiled like he'd just won the lottery. "She is Venitia Marietto. Venitia *Pizziani* Marietto. I have called her for you. She knows everyone." He handed me a piece of paper with an address on it. "She will meet you today at the fountain. By the Palazzo di Mozart on Via St. Catherine. She will wear a purple scarf."

I had no idea where this fountain or palazzo place was, but I didn't care. We had a lead and, based on what I could see on the Google maps, Ala was tiny. *"Buono. Grazie,"* I said, blowing Pietro a kiss.

Grams and Pen waved. The bomber boys saluted.

"Okay, girls and boys," I said as I settled behind the wheel of our rental car. "Cross your fingers. Here goes nothing."

Grams clenched her purse. "What boys? Where are we going again?"

I glanced at Pen and the boys in the rearview mirror. Was Grams messing with me or did she really not know? "We're on a mission, Grams," I said. "We have to see a lady about your Bish."

As I drove along the highway bordering the Adige River near Ala, we passed a rail bridge that sparked memories of Bish's messed up strafing run. I imagined bombs falling on the bridge, and rail lines exploding. On instinct, I swerved to miss flying debris. Pen shrieked, snapping me out of my trance.

"If you're trying to get rid of us," said Bish. "You'll get your wish soon enough. But right now, we have to find a woman about a church."

I blinked. Shook off the vision of fallen bodies. Got my eyes refocused on the road. But deep down, I realized, I was scared to be there. Scared of what we'd find. It must have shown on my face because Grams reached out to touch my arm as I exited the Autostrada and cruised into Ala.

"Holy shit," Pen said when we parked the car and set out on foot through the narrow maze of stone streets that wound through the old part of Ala. Everywhere we looked, there were tall, shuttered buildings, hidden fountains, saintly statues, and bicycles.

Ala. I breathed the place in and practically floated in the fresh mountain air. I couldn't believe we were finally, actually, totally, amazingly there—in Ala. It wasn't just a name in Bish's diary or on some map. It was real. Even Bish and the bomber boys stood in the center of the square, mouths gaping.

"Sure looks different from the ground," said StuBoy. "And how."

Pen put on her sunglasses. "It's all so mysterious and glamorous," she said, sliding one arm through Grams's and one through mine.

Grams smiled as she took in the stone buildings and the fountain in the middle of the square. "Magical. So what are we doing here?"

"We're meeting a lady," I explained again. I'd become so used to reminding Grams about stuff that her redundant questions had almost stopped bugging me. "Venitia Pizziani Marietto."

"Dame at 12 o'clock," shouted Valentine. He was balancing on top of the fountain, pointing at a woman emerging from the Palazzo door and wearing an awesome purple-on-purple zebra striped scarf. Piano music escaped out the door behind her, trailing her like perfume. Her hair was a dark, curly bob, and she had a slim, elegant figure. As she neared us, the lines on her face and the careful confidence of her walk suggested that she was much older than she appeared from a distance.

"Venitia?" I said as the woman approached the fountain. "Venitia Pizziani?"

Venitia smiled and scanned our group. "Sylvie?"

I waved.

"Ah," said Venitia, looking at me. "Pietro said you had the blonde hair and a war coat."

I fingered the zipper on Bish's coat. "Thank you so much for meeting us."

Venitia stood back and took a long look at the bomber jacket. Her eyes went distant, but she snapped out of it as Grams introduced herself and Pen. Venitia smiled at them. Her tailored silk suit shimmered in gold and peach tones as she reached out to take their hands. Teardrop-shaped gold and pearl earrings hung from Venitia's ears. The boys were entranced. Heck, we were all entranced.

"Holy smokes. She's Italy's answer to Audrey Hepburn, if you ask me," said Valentine.

StuBoy nodded. "Mmmm-hmm. Never mind that she must be sixty-some years old."

"You seen Sophia Loren lately?" said Valentine. "She's still a looker and she's older than dirt."

I hissed at them.

"The girls have led us on a wild goose chase," said Grams. "We're grateful for your help."

"No journey of the heart is 'chasing the goose' as you say," said Venitia, pulling off her sunglasses. "But where is the papa?" she asked. "Pietro said this was the mission of the papa."

"My grandfather died about a year ago," I said. "But we're really here for someone who died a long time ago, in the war. I promised we'd finish his last mission."

Venitia tilted her head, let an earpiece of her sunglasses rest on her deep plum lower lip, and raised one dark brown, perfectly shaped brow. "Tell me of this mission?" she said with a question in her voice. "Pietro said you were looking for a church, but also the family of a little girl. She was shot, no?"

I nodded. "Yes, best as we can figure," I glanced toward Bish. "It happened near the train station."

Venitia bit the arm of her sunglasses. "The train station is across the town, by the river. My studio is near there. The churches are here."

"We have to find the oldest chapel," Bish said into my ear. He'd been at my side like a guard dog the whole time. "One with a deep hole."

"Do any of them have a well?" I asked. "A place where you can throw in a blessing or a prayer?"

Venitia paused, frowning.

"We made a *lamella* for the little girl," I said. "A *preghiere*." I stumbled on the Italian.

Venitia smiled. "A prayer, yes."

I nodded. "We heard the ancient Greeks and Romans tossed them in the sea or in a well or a deep crevice." I opened the little bag that hung around my neck and showed Venitia the tiny aluminum prayer note. "The boy who shot her hoped for forgiveness, but he died before he could come here and ask for it himself."

Venitia put her hand to her mouth and let out a small cry. "I see. This is a very important mission. Come, I take you to the *santuario di Sant Marie.*"

I didn't think it was possible for ghosts to be weak kneed, but Bish stumbled when we started along after Venitia. StuBoy reached for Bish's arm and steadied him. Bish shrugged him off. "I'm fine," he said.

"You're one brave SOB," said Valentine. "Most fellas don't have the stomach."

StuBoy clapped Bish on the back. It's weird how women hug and men thump to show each other support.

When we arrived at the small chapel, Venitia put her scarf over her head and pulled another out of her purse to cover Pen's bare shoulders. Both of them made the sign of the cross before entering, and I was amazed at how the unspoken Catholic rituals resurfaced in Pen's renegade brain. I felt like an interloper but knew more than anything that I needed to walk with Grams and Bish into this sacred place. Grams was studying the vaulted ceilings, the simple frescoes, the carved column tops when I took her arm. Bish was right there with us.

Venitia headed toward the altar, but surprised us by stepping into an alcove at the side and slipping down a set of narrow stone stairs. "The *chiesa* was built on top of an ancient temple," she said, leading us toward a small hearth carved from the stone. "We hid down here sometimes during the war." A deep crack had split the stone hearth, and remnants of carved stone cornucopias decorated each side. "It cracked here, long before my life, so deep they have never found its end."

"Holy shit," said Penelope, her voice echoing around the crypt. She quickly covered her mouth when Grams gave her The Look. "Sorry."

"This is good," Bish whispered as he ran a hand over the two-inch crack. "Leave the prayer here."

"The well is deep with prayers," said Venitia. "Yours would be welcome."

"Sylvie, go on," Grams urged.

I knelt at the hearth and fished the tiny roll of aluminum out of my necklace bag one last time. "Bish said the original was gold, but the message was the same." Grams knelt next to me, then Pen. Venitia tried to slide toward the back of the room, but I motioned her forward and we made room for her between us. "Without you, Venitia, we wouldn't be here," I said, pulling Bish's picture out of my photo book and setting it upright at the back of the shallow altar.

Venitia's breath caught in a weird way when she saw Bish's picture. Grams sniffed, and placed one hand on Venitia's arm, the other on mine. Bish and the boys hovered close behind us.

Silence seeped through the ancient stones and wrapped us in its blanket. I closed my eyes and held the prayer note above the hearth crack. The words I'd memorized like forever ago burbled up from somewhere inside of me to get Bish started.

"Please God, grant me forgiveness," I began.

I shot a little girl. Bish's voice echoed in my head.

"I'd like to think it was an accident—
That I couldn't see her until it was too late,
That my hand was too trained on the trigger."

Our voices filled the chamber.

*But I saw her face. Saw her kneeling
By her broken and bloody mother,
Saw her pleading eyes, and shot her anyway.*

*She irreplaceable.
I despicable.
And yet I live.*

*I would forfeit my own daughter or granddaughter
If ever you saw fit to give me either, to right this wrong.
I never thought the face of this war could be so young,
So full of fear. So familiar.*

Please help that little girl know I'm sorry.

"So, so sorry," Bish whispered.

The prayer note slid between my fingers and made a soft scraping sound as it fell into the sacred crack. Venitia leapt to her feet. *"Mi scusi,"* she said, hurrying out of the crypt. We all swapped worried looks. Grams wiped tears from her eyes, and Pen dashed up the stairs after Venitia. StuBoy rubbed his face and followed them out.

In the flickering candlelight, I looked at Grams. "We did it. I can't believe after all this, we did it." I buried my face in her shoulder and she wrapped her arms around me. We hugged long and hard. Yet underneath this moment of victory, I couldn't stop wondering what had made Venitia run.

CHAPTER TWENTY

THE 50TH MISSION PHOTO

We found Penelope and Venitia at the church entrance. Both were dabbing at their eyes with tissues. Their smiles made me think of days when the sun shines through the rain.

"Come, I will take you to my shop," said Venitia. "It is near the *treno*."

I was dying to ask Pen if she knew what made Venitia so upset back in the crypt, but there was no way to say anything without making it a group discussion. Grams walked alongside Venitia. Despite the fact that Grams couldn't remember where she last put her purse, small talk and distant memories were no problem. Very weird.

Venitia asked Grams how she knew Bish. I tried to listen in, but Pen slid back to walk with me, looping her arm through mine.

"Hey, girl," she said as our feet slapped along the narrow stone street. "Mission accomplished. Way to go."

"That's right," said Bish. "Couldn't have done a better job myself."

I flashed a twisted smile. "I don't know. Venitia seemed pretty upset. Did she say anything to you?"

Pen shrugged. "When I found her, she was kneeling in a pew whispering something in Italian, '*Perdonare, dimenticare. Perdonare, dimenticare,*' or something like that, over and over."

"God, we must seem like such freaks to her."

"What I couldn't figure out was why would she say that and not the usual, 'Bless me, Dude, for I have sinned'," said Pen.

"How do you know that's not what she was saying?"

"Because I looked it up in the phrase book and 'bless' is *benedire.*" Pen leaned in and whispered. "I think she knows the family and that's why she's all emotional."

My fingers fumbled with the zipper of Bish's bomber jacket. Up and down. "Really Pen, it could be anything. We'll just wait for the right time and ask."

The boys stopped dead in their tracks when we got to the railway station.

"It's been rebuilt since we blasted the hell out of it," Bish said.

"But I'll be damned if the stone house next door isn't still exactly the same," said Valentine.

"And how," said StuBoy. "All that's missing are the burning trucks out front and the scattered bodies. We'd be standing on them right now."

"Eeuuw," I said. "TMI." Pen gave me the I-know-they-said-something-so-tell-me look, so I did.

"Oh my god, I can smell it," Pen said. "Fire, death."

"Try wood smoke and sewage treatment plant," I said, pointing to the industrial area on the other side of the train tracks.

Pen snarled at me and I almost missed Bish puking into a garbage can. StuBoy and Valentine caught him by the coat collar, and I found myself dashing forward to Grams and Venitia. *"Mi scusi,* Venitia. I'm sorry, but I have to ask. Do you know the family of this little girl?"

Venitia tensed as if a sharp pain had seared her back. She covered it with a smile. "It is, how do you say, complicated. My office is just this way. Please. We can sit and talk. Have an espresso. Then I try to answer your questions."

Pen caught up and attempted to lighten the mood. "All I really want to know is where you got that rockin' scarf," she said. "I dream about accessories like that."

Venitia laughed. "I will show you," she said to Penelope. "The shop is just here." She pointed to a stone and glass high-style storefront, then put her arm around my shoulders. "I'm sorry I do not answer your question right away, but you surprise me." She pulled one of the glass doors open and shooed us inside. Bolts of silk velvet hung everywhere. Gold, purple, red, burnt orange, and butter yellows hung with blues and greens so deep they looked like slices of the sea. Venitia led us to a glass conference room and asked her assistant to bring a round of espressos.

"My family has been in the silk trade for generations," said Venitia. "They planted many of the trees for the worm."

"That's why I've seen so many Mulberry trees around here," said Grams. She often surprised me with what she remembered. Like tree names. "Of course."

"The only thing we ever used silk for was parachutes," said StuBoy.

"I always wanted one of those fancy silken bow ties," said Bish.

"Forget the tie, make mine silk underwear." Valentine smiled and wiggled his eyebrows. "With a gal in them."

"Oh, shut up," I whispered without realizing I was speaking and giggling out loud. Pen slapped me and made the others think she had told me a joke.

Grams looked at me like she knew my secret. "Why don't you show Venitia your art journal," she said.

"She doesn't need to see it," I said. "It's okay."

"The hell she doesn't," said Bish. "We didn't come all this way to give up now. Listen to your grandmother."

"Sylvie, we all need to see it," said Pen.

There was something in her tone that I couldn't ignore. I put the art journal on the table and flipped it open to where I'd jotted down what I remembered of Bish's *signadora* story. Opposite the last page, I'd drawn and collaged the very image that had haunted Bish—and me—for weeks: A little girl's face, eyes wide and fierce, among the wreckage of war.

Pen's eyes popped. "God Syl, what a creepy picture," she blurted. "Oh, sorry." Pen cringed when she saw Venitia move in for a closer view.

"Venitia, this is the reason we're here," I explained. "This is the little girl Bish killed. He needed us to deliver the prayer note—to ask forgiveness for what he did. We want to try to find her family—to say how sorry we are that she was killed. How sorry I am that my grandfather bombed your town."

Venitia shook her head, her eyes blinking long and hard. *"Mi scusi,"* she said, stepping out of the conference room. "I must find one thing."

My hand slid along the edge of Bish's jacket, fingertips on the soft lining. I turned to Grams. "Is my middle name Bishop because of Bish? I've been wondering."

Clouds formed in Grams's eyes. "Does it really matter?"

"Yes," Pen and I said in unison.

Grams covered her face in her hands and crumpled into the chair I pulled out for her. "I wish I knew. Oh, how I wish I knew," she said, her voice cracking. "I keep trying to remember these things, but just when I think I have them, they scatter like mice. Chuck adopted you, Bernadette. He was your father. I had to forget Bish and move on. I couldn't marry a ghost no matter how much I loved him. I had you to consider."

Bish moved behind Grams in a sort of "protector" position. He reached his hand to her shoulder and left it there. Grams reached for it, natural as anything. Pen glanced at me, questioning. I decided to blow off Grams's mix-up between me and Mom.

"I'm sorry, Merrilee," said Bish. "I'm sorry I messed up and got myself killed. I'm sorry I left you all alone. You're the swellest gal I've ever known. I never could stop loving you."

"He never stopped loving you," I said to Grams. "He was so sorry for leaving you all alone."

"I know, I know," said Grams, sliding behind a veil of tears. I bent down and put my head on Grams's shoulder like I was five again. Grams stroked my hair and I got a soothing whiff of her Emeraude perfume.

When I lifted my head, Venitia had returned and was staring at the drawing in my art book. She set a small black-and-white photo on it, and I was stunned to see that the little girl in the photo was a twin to the one in my journal.

"This drawing is extraordinary," said Venitia.

"That photo is freaky," said Pen.

"This girl," Venitia said to me. "How did you know her?"

I shrugged. Bit my lip. Opted for a version of the truth. "I don't know her. I'm sorry. I saw her in a dream. A vision."

Venitia eased out her breath and raised her large dark eyes to mine.

"Holy cow," Bish whispered behind me.

Then I, too, realized I knew those eyes. Sixty years had hardly changed them.

"Number one, Sylvie. Do not apologize," said Venitia. "Your grandfather liberated our town. Freed us from the Germans who had occupied our houses, our land—hunted and killed the men who fought for our freedom. Do not be sorry."

Venitia looked from me to my drawing. "And yes, I do know the family of this little girl."

"Who? Where are they?" cut in Pen, her eyes like flying saucers and her lime green peace earrings on the sway.

I stopped fingering the jacket lining and swallowed hard. "Please, Venitia, tell us how to find them." My voice came out all spluttery. "We have to tell them Bish didn't mean to kill her. She was kneeling by this lady and ran into his line of fire. He didn't mean to shoot her. It was an accident. After that he was very, very sick. The *signadora* said it was the evil eye. She was the one who told him to come here. To deliver the prayer."

Venitia seemed to melt into a chair. Grams reached over and put her hand on Venitia's. Venitia squeezed Grams's hand, then let go to make the sign of the cross. "Is he here now?" Venitia asked.

I bit my lip and nodded, uncertain how she'd take it.

Venitia smiled. She nodded. She was elegant even when accosted by us nosy Americans. "Here, we believe the spirits are all around us," she said. "And the evil eye is very real."

Grams unfolded and refolded her hands. "Oh, dear," she said.

Venitia surprised us all by untying her scarf. "I want you all to know something. Your lover, your grandpapa, he didn't kill this little girl."

Pen and I did a major double take. "How do you know?" I asked.

Venitia gave a weak smile, shrugged one shoulder. "Because she is me."

Penelope shrieked. Bish bit his lip and squeezed his eyes closed. When he opened them, Venitia lifted her hand from her heart and unbuttoned the top button of her V-necked blouse. She pulled the collar to one side.

"Oh, dear," exclaimed Grams. "You poor thing."

A jagged scar ran from her neck to her collarbone. Another scar the size of a fifty-cent piece was closer to her arm. "Oh, yes, I was shot, injured badly," Venitia said. "But not killed. I was but *cinque*—five. And all my adult life I have worried that in my child's anger, I had fixed him with the evil eye."

I squeezed my eyes to hold back tears. "You did, but he recovered. Mostly."

Pen blew her nose. "But didn't you just hate him for bombing you? For destroying your village, and nearly destroying you? I would have."

Venitia tilted her head toward Pen. "My dear, you have no idea how my people suffered under *tedesca*, the men of Hitler. They took our homes, our food, killed our families, anyone who went against them. I was a child, not knowing that these Americans were freeing us from them. But now I see that you have suffered too."

"There's been too much suffering," said Grams. "That's why we're here. To put things right before I am too old and can't remember."

Venitia nodded. "May I ask you a question?"

"Of course," Grams and I said in unison. Pen coughed. She always said I sounded more and more like Grams every summer.

"What was his name?" said Venitia. "Your lover. The man who did this to me?"

My eyes swiveled toward Grams. "His name was Keith Bishop," she said. "But everyone called him Bish."

Venitia stood. "Where is he?"

I pointed to Grams. "Right behind her." I rummaged in my bag and got the goggles. "Here, try these," I said, handing them to Venitia. "If you believe we are surrounded by spirits, then these may help you see."

"Okay, Bish," said StuBoy. "Now's your chance."

Venitia slid on the goggles. She gazed around the room playfully, then gasped. *"Mi scusi! Mi scusi,"* she said as she and Bish locked eyes for the second time in their lives.

"I'm sorry, Venitia," said Bish.

"Sono dolente," whispered Venitia.

For a second, I saw Bish and Venitia as they were sixty-something years ago. Only this time, Bish was a young hero come to liberate her village and little Venitia represented his whole reason for fighting the war. Forgiveness passed between them, unspoken but completely understood. My legs went wobbly with the intensity of it. Somewhere outside, bells rang; A church bell struck three times.

"Oh, damn," said StuBoy. "We're down to three. This is real sweet and all, but if we're not at the Maria Dolens by sunset, Death wins."

"What's the Maria Dolens?" I asked StuBoy, not thinking about the fact that Grams and Pen couldn't hear him.

Venitia slid the goggles up to her forehead and turned to me. "Come, I show you."

Chapter Twenty-One

The Lamella

I gave Venitia the keys as we hurried to the rental car. "Here, you drive. You know the way." Since I'd been driving illegally in the eyes of the rental company, it didn't seem like a big deal to add one more.

We crammed into the car, Pen and Grams in the back, Venitia and I in the front. The bomber boys rode rodeo style on top. They whooped when Venitia made the tires squeal as we pulled out of the parking lot.

"Now who is this Maria Dolens?" asked Pen.

Venitia rounded a corner and merged onto the Autostrada headed north toward Rovereto. "It's not a someone. It's, how do you say, *campana dei caduti?* The bell of the fallen."

"Seriously? It's a bell?" said Pen. "How boring is that? I thought it was some hot chick."

"No, no," said Venitia. "It is a bell such as you have never seen."

"Then what's the big rush?" Pen looked over the top of her sunglasses. "Is it going somewhere?"

"No," said StuBoy, popping his head through the roof. "We are."

"The bell, it was made from the war cannons," said Venitia. "To acknowledge all the peoples who died in wartimes."

StuBoy stuck his head through the roof again. "It's even more than that, and how. It's our runway to the other side, to Headquarters."

His comment made me choke. It was one of those weird moments when you realize that even though you're getting what you thought you wanted, you don't want it anymore. I didn't want Bish and the boys to go. Without them, the here and now felt boring and claustrophobic. Without them, I went back to being Nobody Special.

As we drove northward, the road twisted and turned deeper into the rising mountains. I started to twitch, looking for flak guns.

"Remember all those flak guns all along the hillside above town?" I heard StuBoy say up top.

"How could we forget them?" said Valentine.

"It was like flying into a damn hornet's nest," Bish said.

As I stared out the car window into the lush countryside, it was hard to imagine the place at war. Rovereto spilled gracefully from the mountainside. Trees surrounded it in tufts of green, and the River Adige made a snaky border along the west side of town. There was no sign of wartime damage—the bridges and train yards the boys had bombed showed no sign of attack. Maybe people heal their war wounds by fixing things.

My gut spun when we finally turned off the Autostrada and wound up a hill outside of town to the Maria Dolens parking lot. It was an amazing clear day and we could see out over the hills, over the town of Rovereto and north to the mountains.

"Just think, Syl," Valentine said when he jumped off the car roof. "After today, no more bomber boys to bother you."

"That's right," said StuBoy. "Your job is done. Time to celebrate." He and Valentine slapped Bish on the back and raced each other to the bell platform. Bish hung back with me while Pen, Grams, and Venitia chattered on about the stupid bell. I didn't want to hear any of it. I didn't even want to see it.

"I never thought I'd say this, but don't go," I said to Bish as I dragged along behind the girls. We entered a long concrete pathway lined with flagpoles. "Can't you call Headquarters or something and get an extension?"

Bish frowned and shook his head, dug his hands deep into his pockets. "That's not how it works. If I don't report back to Headquarters, I don't get to move on. Don't forget that I waited 60 years for you already." He smiled and winked at me.

Air hissed from between my lips. We walked on in silence.

"Heard you girls mooning over my pictures of Capri," Bish said. He was trying to change the subject, lighten the mood. But he was right. Grams had asked me to stay in Italy with her, to go see some of the places Bish had visited. It would be weird not to have him along.

"Seriously, there's no reason you guys have to go anywhere," I said. "I'm good with having you hang around."

Bish ran an arm through one of the flagpoles. "Sylvie, gal, it's not as if we get a choice," said Bish. "Like it or not, we're spirits, plain and simple. We have to move on. Good or bad, it's part of the deal."

My fingers fumbled with the jacket edge and latched onto something small and cigarette shaped in the lining of the jacket. I slid the tiny object to a hole in the lining and gasped. "Jiminy Crackers, it's been here all along!" Bish and I stopped to gawk at the tiny piece of gold.

"Impossible," said Bish.

Part of me wanted to close my hand around the *lamella*, to guard it forever. The other part wanted to show it to everyone, to prove that it existed. The second part won. "Pen, Grams, Venitia!" I shouted to them. They stopped and turned. "I found it! The real one. It was in his coat lining the whole time." I ran to them and cupped the tiny *lamella* in my palm, holding it out for everyone to see. "It's the prayer note Bish made in the house of the *signadora* all those years ago."

Grams shook her head. "It was there the whole time? Oh, that damn jacket. Such a keeper of secrets. Too many memories. Too much pain." She plucked the tiny piece of gold from my palm and placed it in Venitia's hand, closing her fingers around it. "We've already had Bish's prayer answered by meeting you. I'm sure Bish would want you to have this."

Bish nodded.

"*I* want you to have this." Grams squeezed Venitia's hand.

Venitia blinked. Swallowed hard. When she looked first at Grams, then at me, I didn't see Venitia the 60-something-year-old woman. I saw the little girl who stared back at me from Bish's memory, then later from my dreams. My hands closed around hers too.

"It's the original prayer for forgiveness he meant to bring here so long ago," I said.

Venitia closed her eyes and nodded, pressed our fists to her lips. "Come with me," she whispered.

When we got to the stretch of white plaza where the bell stood, I was blown away. The massive Maria Dolens hung between two stone pillars, forming a sort of gateway some twenty feet tall. Since the bell plaza was nestled into the side of the hill above Rovereto, all we saw beyond the bell was a sweeping view of the valley.

As we moved closer to the bell, I could make out the pictures of soldiers and horses and warriors cast in relief around its lower rim. The raking sun highlighted the characters in the bell's procession— each one represented a different time, a different story.

"*Campana dei caduti*," said Venitia. "The bell of the fallen." She walked to the edge and looked out over a stream that tumbled down the mountainside.

"What a view," said Grams.

"We call this the Wishmaker's Graveyard," said Venitia.

Valentine tossed a worried glance toward the mountains. The sun dangled above an infinite horizon where fields unfurled to meet forests and forests swilled around rock spires.

"Is your Bish here?" Venitia asked.

I nodded. "StuBoy and Valentine too."

"*Buon.*" Venitia turned to us and smiled. "Bish. Sylvie, Merrilee, Penelope, StuBoy, and Valentino. *Grazie.* You have made my heart very happy."

AT THE WISHMAKER'S GRAVEYARD

Venitia threw the lamella off the cliff
As the bell began to swing.
Gently, she kissed each one of us,
Like the bell kissed the warm air—
First one cheek then the next—
And blew a kiss to the bomber boys.
Back to heaven,
Hand to heart,
Two souls healed, redeemed.
A flash,
As the sun beyond the hills bathed
The high arc of a flying prayer
In warm light before it splashed
And sank to the place
Where wishes are answered.

THE MARIA DOLENS

"Sun's setting," said Valentine. "The bell's swinging. Time to get in the queue."

I checked around to see how many people were nearby. I needed to talk to these guys but I didn't want to look like a total whacko talking to thin air. A man walked by gesticulating wildly and spewing Italian—earpiece in action. I so totally wanted to get one of those when I got home. But then I realized I wouldn't need it, because there would be no Bish, no StuBoy, no Valentine.

My heart slowed, threatening to stop.

"Don't be sad, Sylvie," Bish said as I turned away from the group. "We did it. You did it. Better than I ever imagined. Now your grandmother needs you. So I'm gonna get out of your hair."

I nodded, let my shoulders sag. I was tired of people needing me. Not really. Sorta.

Valentine and StuBoy crowded in.

"Hey, Sylvie gal," said Valentine. "It's been an honor to meet you. Knowing you and Penelope has been like having a coupla little sisters."

"Sisters, my eye," said StuBoy, wiping his nose. "I'm in love."

Valentine gave StuBoy a shove.

StuBoy stuffed his hands in his pockets and shuffled his feet. "Sylvie, how about you do a dead guy a favor? Let Pen borrow those goggles. Just this once. I want to know if she can see me."

"But what if she can't?" I said. "She's always so wanted to be the psychic, the clairvoyant, the mystic. She'd be devastated if they didn't work for her."

StuBoy shook his head. "You're wrong Sylvie. I think she could see us *if* she had the goggles. You don't need them. You see us just fine."

I bit my lip as the bell swung higher. The clapper would soon find its mark.

"Damn it, Syl, stop being so selfish." StuBoy's eyes bored into mine. "There will never be another chance."

In the sky, clouds turned into puffs of fresh honey butter. "Where's StuBoy?" Pen asked, moving next to me.

"Right beside you."

Pen jumped right through him.

StuBoy tossed a how-about-now look my way.

"He wants me to give you the goggles. So you can see him."

"Awesome."

"Hurry," insisted StuBoy.

I dug in my bag feeling selfish and stupid, wondering why I hadn't wanted to share this magic with my best friend. Was it because I wanted to be different from she-who-is-so-amazing? Better? To stand apart from such a bright and outgoing personality? Truth is, none of that mattered anymore. I handed Pen the goggles. "StuBoy is right. I'm being selfish not letting you try."

Pen hugged the goggles to her chest, then hugged me.

"Make it quick, girl. We're getting ready for take-off," said Valentine.

We all turned to look out over the Trento Valley as the great bell began to ring.

Pen's hands shook as she pulled the goggles onto her head and over her eyes. "Holy shit!" she exclaimed, spinning around. "Which one is he?"

StuBoy looked confused. Apparently he hadn't noticed the long stream of war-torn men who had appeared behind him since the gianormous bell had begun to ring. "I'm right here," StuBoy said, waving his arms. "With Bish and Valentine. Can you see us?"

"You and about two hundred other guys." I said.

Pen's mouth opened and closed like a goldfish on speed. "It's, it's like a whole other world."

She was right. No way would I have ever have believed it if I hadn't see it. Guys in uniforms walked alongside armored Roman soldiers. World War II gunners in flight suits, camo-covered infantrymen, and boys in bandages limped by, eyes bright with the prospect of finally going home.

Pen stepped closer to StuBoy. "Good thing I couldn't see him before."

"What do you mean?" I asked.

"He's even cuter in real life than in his picture, and I'd have been a goner for sure."

StuBoy laughed. "I guess it's lucky for both of us that this is it, then."

"What did you say?" said Pen, looking sideways at StuBoy.

StuBoy scuffed the toe of his boot into the white stone of the bell plaza.

"He means that's our call," cut in Valentine.

Pen hooted. "Valentine! You look just like your picture."

"They have to go," I said. "Before the bell stops ringing."

"Tell her she's one hell of a girl," said StuBoy.

"Believe it or not, I can hear you just fine," said Pen, locking eyes with StuBoy. They traded sad smiles. Slowly, gently, Pen reached toward StuBoy, one index finger extended. StuBoy held his finger to hers and they stood there for a long, quiet moment, touching or not touching the only way they could. Living people around us stared as if Pen and I were a couple of mime freaks, but the dead who passed by nodded in understanding. There beneath the towers of Maria Dolens, even the air was mystic. As I scanned the grounds, I saw by the quiet wandering of visitors called to the bell that some of the living could feel it too. Grams and Venitia were among them.

The bell picked up speed, finding its rhythm as if it was the world's only heartbeat. We were there, at an airstrip between worlds—a take-off place for all who had been killed in battle— but I could not find my voice to say good-bye.

The sun seemed to grip the horizon, hanging halfway between dark and light.

Valentine tugged at StuBoy and Bish. "Sorry, Penelope, Sylvie Girl, but somebody's gotta keep these wrap-leggings on schedule."

I turned toward Bish. He'd been weirdly quiet the whole time. "Why didn't you warn me? How can you just leave?" I shouted. My knees were wobbly. I was pretty sure someone had shoved a cotton ball down my throat. "Don't go."

Bish stepped toward me, arms wide, but stopped short when a snide voice ripped the air.

"Ah look, it's an American love fest." The voice was unfamiliar but the smug sneer was unmistakable. I remembered the guy from Bish's box, but he had a distinctive strut, a different kind of war-torn uniform.

"Tetro. What the hell are you doing here?" Bish asked. "Last I'd heard, the Air Corps gave you the boot for killing me."

"Hell. I guess they ran outta guys to fight the slanty-eyed dog-eaters," said Tetro. "Shipped me out to fight the Japs. Finally bit it in Korea. Took a damn long time to get here, I'll say." His shifty eyes sized up the bell. "I guess this old piece of lead tolls for everyone. Even brown-nosers like you."

"I shoulda hammered you when I had the chance," said Bish, raising a fist and standing his ground. "They should've court-marshaled you for not clearing those guns."

"Now, now," said Tetro, turning a pouty face to Bish. "I've been payin' up in Pergatory all these years, just so I could say my sorries."

"That's real swell," said Bish as StuBoy and Valentine moved to either side of him. "So you're starting with me?"

"Ending." Tetro hocked up a disgusting loogie. "So, well, ah, sorry then, Bishop," he grumbled before moving toward the bell.

"Too little too late, Tetro," said StuBoy after him.

Tetro turned to salute the bomber boys with his middle finger before disappearing beneath the bell.

"Some fellas never learn," said Valentine, his eyes on the space where Tetro had vanished. He turned to Bish and StuBoy. "Well, boys, we best get this show on the road."

Valentine turned to Pen and me, trying to look sincere, but leaning eagerly toward the bell. "No offense girls, but I'm not getting cooped up in another photograph."

StuBoy smiled at Pen. "Don't think we don't love you girls, but we've been called to other things. Poe's bringing the plane around and we've gotta catch 'er on the next updraft."

Bish was quiet, hands shoved deep into his pockets. Everything in me wanted to grab him and make him stay. I didn't want to lose another grandfather, even if he was only a 19-year-old ghost. "Don't go," I said. "Please don't go."

Valentine put one hand on StuBoy's shoulder, the other on Bish's. "Been one hell of a ride, girls."

The Maria Dolens's toll seemed to shatter my eardrums. Bish broke free of his buddies and touched my arm. "You are the swellest granddaughter a fella could ever have. I never could have dreamed up a better gal—aside from Merrilee, that is." He looked at Grams who was mesmerized by the setting sun.

"Then stay," I pleaded. "She needs you. I need you."

Bish leaned in next to my ear, so close I'd swear I could feel his stubble. "Don't worry, I'll see you again. Sometime when you least expect it."

Pen pushed back the goggles. "I can't see anymore," she said.

I took the goggles and realized they were all teary and steamed up.

"Thank you, Sylvie," said Bish. "And Penelope. I never would have made it if it weren't for you too." He leaned over and kissed first her cheek, then mine.

A breeze slid across the landing. I tugged Bish's bomber jacket tight around me as the sun slipped farther into the horizon, leaving only its narrow, fiery crown. Pen wiped the goggles on her shirt and put them back on. Death crept out from behind the mountains, black as night. With it came a strange, distant rumbling of propellers. Stu-Boy and Valentine turned to follow the last ghostly stragglers toward the bell. Bish trailed behind them, Grams trailed after him.

When the guys neared the ringing, swaying bell, the rumble of engines grew so loud it drowned out the Maria Dolens. The living covered their ears and looked to the sky. The bomber boys paused and turned. Valentine saluted. StuBoy blew Pen a kiss. Bish glanced back at Grams, then hurried away.

As the boys disappeared and the bell slowed, the rumbling moved off into the night.

"It's Pippo!" someone in the crowd said. "The ghost plane."

I reached for Pen, Grams, and Venitia as the sun flashed and Death swallowed its fire. In that flash, I saw Bish's bomber circle one last time.

"That's the way I want to go," said Grams. "Just disappear into the sunset."

A sweet scent rose up from the deep valley to meet us. "Ah, the oleander," Venitia said, breathing the valley air.

Pen wiped away her tears, and the four of us laced arms to silently say our last good-byes.

"What will we do now, without Bish and the boys?" I said, burying my head in Grams's shoulder.

Grams hugged me close, reached up ever-so-gently to pick the stray bangs out of my eyes. "We go on," she said, glancing at Venitia. "We make the best of things."

CHAPTER TWENTY-THREE

PICTURES OF CAPRI

Grams, Pen, and I made the best of things by bumping back our flight by a couple days and taking off for the island of Capri. Grams figured that if Bish could take rest leave there, so could we. We tried to talk Venitia into coming with us, but she had work to do and a business to run. She gave each of us an amazing silk scarf. "Something to remember me by," she said. As if we'd ever forget her.

It felt weird to be on our own, without the bomber boys, without a mission. Things were way too quiet.

"Have you called your mom yet?" Pen asked when we stepped off the ferry at Marina Grande. "She's probably freaking out."

"No doubt she would if she actually knew we were here," I said. "But what she doesn't know can't hurt her. Besides, I told the people at Grace that Grams was staying at Kate's for a few days, and Kate and Mom think I'm with Grams. Which I am. So it's all good, right?"

Boat horns blew, and the air smelled of salt and fish.

"Just hope your mom doesn't call my dad. I told him your mom was meeting us here in Italy." Pen scanned the open boats in the marina, eyes eager. "That's the only reason he let me come."

"I want to go swimming," said Grams.

"You and me both," said Pen.

It was around two o'clock in the afternoon and sweat trickled down the side of my face. I wanted to find the beach where Bish had been. The one in his photos.

I spotted the entrance to the funicular, the little red cable car that carried people up and down the steep island hill to and from Capri town. "Let's drop our stuff at the hotel, then hit the beach," I said. We tugged our wheelie bags along the stone wharf, getting sweatier by the second.

The island map I picked up on the ferry crinkled in my hand as we stepped off the funicular. "The hotel is this way." I motioned to Pen and Grams as we entered a small plaza where window boxes overflowed with flowers. "Hotel Bonaventura."

"This place is magic," said Grams. Her short gray hair skipped across her forehead in the warm island breeze. Even though she usually wilted in the heat, her eyes gleamed like deep blue sea glass. She fingered the vines of lush pink flowers that spilled over rock walls as if amazed that they were real. Bright blue flowers that looked like bursting fireworks edged the stone-paved entryways. It was as if we'd walked into a fairy tale village.

We passed a white archway with "Hotel La Palma" spelled out on it in gold letters. "Hey Grams, that's the hotel Bish wrote about," I said, pointing to the white archway. A nearly life-size golden bull marked the shaded entrance. The interior, what we could see of it, was a blend of swanky modern. I got Bish's diary and started reading out loud like it was a guidebook to the island.

17 MAGGIO–May; MARTEDI–Tuesday

Went to the La Palma Hotel and had dinner. Danced with Mayme LaMontero from Connecticut. She's a civilian worker at Naples. She's pretty well built, but not much in the brain class.

Pen snorted.

"Apparently he liked smart girls like you, Grams," I said. "But what was he doing dancing with some other chick?"

"Oh, he loved to dance," said Grams. "He was good at it too. We danced for hours that last night we had together."

I bet they did.

Pen peeked around the hotel porch and down the narrow street. "I see our hotel," she said. "Come on, it's this way."

A few steps later, we were at the hotel and I was showing the clerk Bish's photo album. Next I flipped open my map of the island. *"Ad dove?"* I asked, pointing from a picture of Bish on the beach to the map. "Do you know where this picture was taken?"

The guy was older, balding, and didn't speak much English, but he got the idea and marked the location of Bish's beach on my map. "Marina Piccolo," he said.

Fifteen minutes later, we were on the move.

"I've never seen so many women in white pants," said Pen. "And those heels. I have to get some of those Italian heels."

"On these stones? I don't know how they do it." The whole scene was making me feel like a hick, so I tried to stay on task. "The road to the beach is over there," I pointed to a sign that said "Via Krupp." The "road" was so narrow, it was no wonder Capri didn't allow cars.

"Oh, Sylvie, look at these." Grams had wrapped herself in a whirl of super cute sundresses hanging in an open shop on the square. "Pick one out. Both of you. My treat."

We left the shop wearing new sundresses and stylin' Capri sandals. "You girls are such fun," said Grams. "You look beautiful." Her eyes changed like a spring sky; clouded and sad one second, clear and sunny the next.

Pen and I hugged Grams and swept her along to the Via Krupp. The big bright beach bag Grams had purchased along with our dresses hung over my shoulder and was weighed down with towels, sunscreen, books, snacks, my journal, and Bish's book of pics snapped sixty years before. We passed the Garden of Augustus and started down the switchbacks that led to the water's edge.

"Look at that color," said Grams, taking in the rock-edged turquoise water far below. "Makes me want to dive right in."

"Wait till we're a little closer," I said, winking at her.

As we walked, Pen put her hand on my shoulder. "Don't you think you should at least check your phone to see if you have any messages?"

I rolled my eyes at her. "Since when was it your job to worry about my messages?"

"Since I wouldn't be able to stand it. My dad has texted me like everyday, just to see if I'm still alive."

"It's only been four days."

"Think about it the other way," said Pen. "What if something happened to your mom or your aunt and the babies? Wouldn't you want to know?"

She had a point. Besides I didn't have the no-service excuse because Mom had always made a point of getting a phone plan that allowed us to talk internationally. "Blah, blah, blah, blah," I mouthed to Pen as I dug my phone out of the bag and turned it on. Everything had been moving so quickly I hadn't even missed it. Maniac beeping filled the air as soon as it hooked up with its homeport or whatever alien satellite controlled it.

Pen was right, there were like 27 messages from Mom. The latest being:

"Where are you? Kate and I are frantic. Grace Retirement said Grandma left with you four days ago. Text me ASAP."

Crap. She wasn't supposed to know we were gone until we got back. "Guess we're in deep doo-doo now, Grams," I said, showing her the text.

Grams grumbled. "No matter what she says, I'm not going back to that Grace Jail. I'd rather jump off a cliff."

The determination on Grams's face was kind of disturbing. There were plenty of cliffs around. In fact, right then we were on one with lots of jagged rocks below. "Don't think you need to get that drastic," I said.

Grams shrugged. "You know how she is. She has to control everything. Call all the shots."

Wow. Grams was more annoyed with her than I'd even imagined.

Pen grabbed Grams and me, making us stop so she could stare us in the eyes. "At least text her to say you're okay. For all she knows, you could be dead."

"We're gonna be when she finds out where we are."

"Do it. Or I will," Pen growled.

"Oh, my," said Grams. "She means business."

"Fine," I said, sneering at Pen. "We're fine," I texted back to Mom. Before she could reply, I shut off the phone and shoved it into the bag.

Our sandals slapped at the stones as we walked along in silence. One zig-zag after another brought us closer to the water and Marina Piccolo.

"Don't be angry, you two," said Grams. "Life is too short, and friends are too precious."

"I'm not angry," said Pen, shrugging one shoulder and looking totally snarky. "I got what I wanted." She smiled and batted her eyes, but I knew it was a show.

"You're such a royal pain-in-the-ass," I said from behind her.

"But you love me anyway." Pen flashed a cheesy smile at me.

Grams reached for my hand as we rounded a tight curve in the path and came to a series of long, low steps. We spotted the distinctive zigzag roofline of the beach huts in Bish's picture way before we got there.

"My goodness," said Grams. "Those black-and-white pictures don't do the place justice. The color—all those aquas, greens, and yellows. The reds and oranges. They practically make my heart stop. Who'd have ever thought?"

Grams was right. The color was awesome. It was a good thing we were holding each other up, because we were both wobbly kneed with the sheer amazement of being there at the one last place where Bish played all those years ago.

As we neared Marina Piccolo, Grams spotted a tiny church and let go of my arm to slide beneath its white stucco arch and through its open doors. Although not as fancy as the churches we'd seen on the mainland, this little church seemed to vibrate with life. A plaque near the door said "Chiesa di Sant'Andrea" which by then I was able to translate to "Church of Saint Andrew." But it wasn't until my eyes adjusted to the low light that I spotted the fish swimming around the chapel in carved wood and stone.

"Whatdya bet Andrew's the patron saint of fishermen?" I said.

"Bingo," said Pen. "We have a winner."

Grams nodded and grinned as she headed over to a small altar filled with candles. Two were burning and a small bin of unused ones sat at the end of the altar. "Come here, Sylvie," she said. "We should each light a candle for Chuck."

I did a double take. "And Bish," I said.

"And Bish, of course."

"And StuBoy," said Pen. "And Valentine."

"Right," I said, even though I felt a bit like we were invading. "But we're not Catholic."

"The dude up at the big house doesn't care," said Pen. "And he's the boss."

My sandals slapped at the churchy quiet as I walked across the cut-marble floor. Grams handed me a short, squat candle and motioned for me to light it, as she did, from one of the two burning candles.

"Please bless Chuck's soul," said Grams, her head down and eyes closed. "Please forgive me for not getting help for him sooner, for sending him to the wrong hospital."

"It wasn't your fault, Merrilee," a familiar voice said. "Chuck went as he was meant to."

Grams raised her eyes as Bish appeared out of the darkness. He was still young and handsome, but he looked older, more serious. "I should have demanded that they get a cardiologist faster," said Grams. "He'd still be alive if I had." I couldn't tell if she saw and heard Bish or was just talking to some greater power.

"Not true," said Bish. "He could have died on the operating table, or worse—been an invalid for the rest of his days. Not Smitty's style." Bish put his hand on Grams's shoulder. She dropped her chin and leaned into his touch, solid in that moment. Clearly she knew he was there.

I glanced at Pen. Her eyes were closed.

Bish caressed Grams's cheek. "Believe it or not, we don't get to choose our times, only our regrets. The only thing I ever regretted was not getting to spend my life with you."

Grams kissed his hand.

Teenage chatter rolled through the open door, shattering the moment. Pen and I turned to see silhouettes in the doorway.

"Someone's in here," called out Pen.

"Sorry," a voice said, retreating. *"Mi squeezie."* Annoying giggles.

When I turned back, Bish was gone and Grams looked as if she'd dropped 40 years.

"I'm sorry I'm such a overbearing Scorpio," said Pen.

I twisted up my lips and nodded. "I'm sorry I'm such a stubborn cow."

"Let's go swimming," said Grams.

CHAPTER TWENTY-FOUR

MARINA PICCOLO

"You're on, baby," I said. We raced through the doorway into the late afternoon sun.

As we scoped around for the bright huts we saw from up on the path, we found a narrow stone passageway that led to the entrance of the pay beach. An oldish guy, tanned and lean, sat near a toll-booth-size office. I showed him Bish's photo album, pointing first at the beach picture, then at the huts. He nodded and smiled, his English about as good as Pen's Italian.

"*Si, si,*" he said, waving to a young guy in a red t-shirt who came running.

"Yummy," said Pen when the guy trotted up the steps. The word SALVATORE was printed in big white letters across the front of his shirt. He rattled off something in Italian to the old guy, who looked at Grams and smiled, pointing to the girl in one of the photos.

"No," said Grams, shaking her head. "She's not me. Should have been, but no."

"That girl didn't last the ferry ride back," I told Salvatore. The old guy flipped the page of the photo book, talking and gesturing wildly when he got to another Marina Piccolo photo. He pointed to some boats in Bish's picture and then to the boathouse down on the beach. Two other guys in red t-shirts stood on duty down there.

"He say we have those since ever," Salvatore pointed at some kayaks in the picture of the beach. "In the boathouse." Bish had written in his diary about trying a kayak for the first time right there at Marina Piccolo. "They no longer seaworthy, but still here."

For a second, it seemed eerie and strange that we were actually there—at the beach where Bish had been just days before he died. Nervous sweat trickled down my back, and when I blinked, I got a little wave of vertigo. Thankfully, Pen set my world right by chatting up Salvatore and the old guy and getting us into the beach for the screamin' deal of five euros each.

Salvatore walked us down to the beach and pointed to a row of green and white striped lounges edging the water. Under our feet, tiny pebbles shifted and rolled. Above us was a deck lined with lounge chairs and the row of bright beach huts. The water was clear and tantalizing under the hot sun. Grams choose a lounge under an umbrella. Pen and I picked lounges on either side in the sun. "This is awesome." I whispered to Grams.

"I go back to watch," said Salvatore.

"Bye," said Pen. She blew him a kiss and he actually seemed to blush under all that tan.

Once we were settled, I scanned the phrase book. When I found the word "salvatore," things began to click. "Pen," I said. "Salvatore isn't his name, it's his job. He's a lifeguard."

"All the better," she said, pursing her lips and looking toward the beach entrance. "Now he can rescue me."

"StuBoy would be so jealous," I kidded.

"Hey, *he* dumped me. A girl's gotta move on. Taste another flavor of gelato."

"You girls are something else," said Grams.

When we waded into the gentle swells, we found that the beach was short and the water beyond deep. No wonder they had a line of swimming buoys strung out around the beach. Pen and I swam out to the buoys and over to the big rock that divides the pay beach from the free beach. Grams seemed happy to splash around in the gentle swells at the shore. From a distance, her retro polka dot one-piece made it seem like she had just stepped out of Bish's picture into our time.

Pen swam to where I was perched on the rock. "Isn't it all just so beautiful and romantic?"

"Hell yeah," I said. "I so wish Grams could have been here with Bish. I'm finally realizing how great they must have been together. I didn't want to believe it at first because of Grandpa Chuck, but Bish was cool."

"It's so awesome you were able to do this for her," said Pen.

"You mean we were able to do this for her," I said. "I couldn't have pulled this off without you. All this makes me wish Grams didn't have to go back."

Pen frowned. "Wishing is a waste of time. Gotta start living." She pushed off the rock, and swam toward where her Salvatore was posted on guard, watching.

The words sounded brutal, but she was right. I dove into the water and swam back to Grams.

"Sylvie dear, there you are," she said. "I've been looking all over for you." She took my hand in hers. "Let's swim." She led me deeper into the water until we were doing the sidestroke, beaming the whole time. When we moved back toward shore where we could stand, Grams looked at the big rock and pointed. "That fellow is sure daring, diving off the rock like that."

I followed her gaze, but didn't see anyone there.

"I want to try." Grams couldn't seem to take her eyes off the rock, and as the sun dropped a little closer to the horizon I saw why. Bish was there, sporting tight U.S. Army green swim trunks. He'd been waving and calling to her.

"Come on, Sylvie. I used to be quite a diver," Grams said just before diving into the water and swimming to the rock. She laughed as Bish took her hand, pulled her up onto the rock with him, and kissed her before diving into the water.

When his head popped out of the swells, Grams smiled and waved.

"Swim with me," called Bish. He smiled his killer smile and opened his arms to her. She stepped toward him, and slipped on the rock.

My breath caught, and before I was waist deep in the water Grams steadied herself and regained her footing. "Grams, wait," I yelled.

She waved at me. "I'm fine," she yelled back. "Watch this." The next moment, she was in the air doing a spectacular swan dive, arms out like wings, then together and plunging into the blue-green water.

I waited for what seemed like forever for her to surface.

When she did, I waved at her, swam toward her. But Bish was there, and she looked different. Short gray hair had gone to long dark brown. Wrinkles had disappeared.

Grams laughed and let Bish nibble at her hand. If I hadn't been so glad to see them young and happy and together, I might have gotten barfy watching them. Bish dropped Grams's arm and swam away, only to appear farther out, waist deep in water. I wondered how he was doing it, then remembered the rocks under the water.

Bish waved and beckoned to Grams. There was something in me that wanted to swim after her, to make her stop, to keep her with me.

Safe. Then I wondered if here with me was safe. Grace Jail may be safe, but she hated it. Everybody said it was for the best, that she'd come to see it that way too. So I started to go after her, but by the time I reached her, she'd already reached Bish. He pulled her up to the top of his rock and they kissed, long and hard.

"Grams!" I called. But in that moment I realized she didn't know me. Not because she'd forgotten, but because I didn't exist in her world. There with Bish, she was seventeen again. Not yet a mother, let alone a grandmother.

"Merrilee!" I shouted and waved. "Don't go."

Grams looked at me and waved. "Who says you can't pick your time?" she said, holding Bish's hand.

"No, Grams!" I swam toward the rock, but before I reached her, she and Bish dove into the water.

I looked around, waiting for them to surface. Nothing. I dove underwater, searching. Back to shore, but Grams was nowhere to be found. "No, no, no, no," I wailed and slapped the water as Pen ran to me.

"Sylvie, what's wrong? I saw you yelling and waving like a crazy girl."

I tasted salt, looked at Grams's empty lounge.

Pen's eyes went wild. "Salvatore! Salvatore!" She waved and screamed, her tie-dye swimsuit swirled through my vision. I heard running, feet on pebbles.

"Di che si tratta?"

Pen sucked air. She pointed at Grams's empty lounge, then at the water. "Holy fuck. What's the Italian word for 'drown'?"

THERE ARE GHOSTS AT THE MARINA PICCOLO

They hide in the blue, green, and yellow striped huts,

They sunbathe on the green and white lounges

Lining the pebble beach.

Grams collected bits of glass and coral scattered among the rocks

She called them "broken memories"—

Edges ground smooth by the hungry sea.

Bish was there. Waiting for sunset
While Death lurked among the rocks.
Grandma smiled and said she saw Bish too.
He'd hooked her heart and made her seventeen again,
Before reeling her into the hungry sea.

There are ghosts at the Marina Piccolo.
They reside in the blue, green and yellow striped huts.
They sunbathe on the green and white lounges
And flirt on the jagged rocks.
Now Grandma is among them, wrapped with Bish
In Death's arms, somewhere beneath the hungry sea.

CHAPTER TWENTY-FIVE

DIAMONDS IN THE SEA

Mom was at a convention in Venice when I finally got hold of her to confess. She was on her way south practically before she hung up. She arrived late that night, and first thing the next morning she was interrogating Salvatore and his red-shirted buddies as they scoured the shoreline beneath the rising sun.

"Why haven't they found her body?" said Mom. "Are you sure she drowned? Maybe she wandered off."

"I saw her dive in," I said. "Salvatore did too."

Salvatore nodded. I think he had run out of English words to explain things to Mom. *"Tutto va bene,"* he said. "We look."

The old guy who just yesterday lounged by the entrance collecting euros stood on a platform down by the beach, yelling commands to the searchers in scuba gear. They knew all the nooks and crannies where the tide hid bodies. They knew the currents, the underwater tunnels and caves that riddled the Capri shores. To me, Death lurked around every corner, transforming Capri from a happy-go-lucky tourist trap to a menacing rock beyond which the sea plunges, deep and secretive. Mostly, I just missed Grams—her hand holding mine, her smile, her disgust with getting old.

As each search hour passed, the men grew less positive, less certain the sea would give up her catch. They spread the word to local fishermen—check your nets. They asked the helicopter pilot who sported tourists around the island to scan the inaccessible shores. They looked at us and said, *"Tutto va bene."* I nodded and smiled. The tendons in Mom's neck stood out more and more as the hours went by.

"We need to let her go," I said as we stood on the beach platform, me gulping water, Mom on the phone with Kate. "Call off the search."

Mom shook her head. She was all tension and demand on the outside, but in her eyes, I caught glimpses of a lost young girl. Nobody, not even my Momclops, wanted to believe moms can die.

"Are the babies okay?" I asked Mom, pointing to the phone.

Mom nodded her head and acted annoyed, but she put her hands together under one cheek. I got it—Kate was still on bed rest.

Mom ranted and paced. *"Tutto va bene.* What the hell is that supposed to mean? If I hear *tutto va bene* one more time I'm going to scream."

"It means 'everything is fine'," said a tall guy with graying longish hair who pulled up in a Salvatore boat to greet the old beach guy. If I were Mom's age, he would be totally hot. The dude's round tortoise-shell glasses made his brown-lashed eyes look big and owlish. His mouth was turned down with concern. "But I guess from the look on your faces this is not true."

Mom paused in her conversation with Kate. "When your mother goes and drowns herself and the searchers can't find her body, it's about as far from fine as one can be."

The man looked at her, then at me. I nodded in agreement.

"Ah, you are them," said the man.

"Them?" Mom's eyes bugged. "Why? What have you heard?"

"Che cosa avete sentito dire? What have I heard, indeed?" He smiled. "The demise of your mother is all over the island. Everyone is at alert, but this is the bad time of year. The currents are angry, the fish are hungry."

"Eeuuw," said Pen.

Mom looked over the top of her designer sunglasses and crossed her arms. "That's really helpful, Mister—ah—?" She took in his tan cargo shorts and faded blue t-shirt.

He tilted his head and shrugged. "Palmero. But you call me Enrico," he added. "It is what it is."

The guy was either super cool or completely whacked. Both options were pretty much okay with me—hell, the dude spoke English. The Salvatore driving the boat said something in Italian and pointed to a big researchy looking boat at the dock. Enrico nodded and held up a finger in the "wait-a-sec" signal.

"Do you know anything? Can you help us?" I said, as Mom went back to Kate. I knew I looked like crap from lack of sleep and the frantic replays of the scene at the beach with Grams and Bish. I wanted everyone to leave Grams alone. "Tell my mom all this searching is useless." The guy stopped and turned.

"Sylvie, get over here," shouted Mom, snapping her phone shut. "The *salvatores* are returning."

I saw a bunch of open-topped boats entering the harbor on the opposite side of Grams's diving rock. Mom ran to the end of the rock. *"Che cosa?"* she shouted. Somebody had told her that was the same as "Anything?" The men shook their heads and held up their empty hands. I glanced at Pen and nodded toward Enrico. We followed him as he took a shortcut down to the beach where the boats were landing. Mom followed us.

"Badare!" one of the lifeguards shouted at Mom as she stepped onto the beach. He motioned for her to step back as they hauled a monster fish out of the boat.

Mom looked like she was going to burst a gasket. "You are supposed to be looking for my mother, not sitting around out there catching fish," she yelled. Her face was bright red and the vein in her forehead looked like a fire hose. "Are you even looking? Do you even care? I can't leave here without her body, without knowing what the hell happened. She has to be out there somewhere. *Capire?"*

"Tutto va bene," said the lifeguard.

Mom closed her eyes and took a deep breath through her nose and exhaled through her mouth like they taught in yoga class.

Enrico called to the lifeguard. They chatted in Italian, then Enrico translated for Mom. "He said the tuna, it came to them while they were looking. Do not be angry." Enrico motioned to the guys hauling the big silver and blue fish across the beach to a fish-gutting table. "We will meet here tomorrow morning to do one last search."

The lifeguard laughed and shouted at Enrico.

Enrico threw up his hands. *"Si debbo.* I cannot refuse to help three beautiful womens." He turned to Pen and me. "You like some espresso? Gelato?"

Mom blinked. "Who can eat gelato at a time like this? The uncertainty of it all makes me intensely nauseous."

She was making me nauseous.

"Your mama," Enrico said to Mom, his big owlish eyes unblinking. "At this time she cannot be saved, only found. Why not the gelato?"

"He has a point," said Pen. She spotted her Salvatore and waved. He waved back, but headed for the group of red shirts huddled around the fish-gutting table.

Enrico and his new entourage, us, moved in the same direction. Mom marched along, fuming. *Domani mattina*—tomorrow morning," she shouted at Enrico. "And every morning after. We will look until we find her."

Enrico shook his head. "If we search too long," he said. "It will anger Neptune. He maybe wish to keep her."

Mom gulped for air. When she spoke again, her voice was small and hesitant. "How often do they find bodies around here?"

"Not so much," said Enrico. "The sea, she has many places for hiding."

It was clear that Mom still didn't want to believe Grams was dead. Enrico paused to lend her a hand as we climbed down off the rocks. Pen's Salvatore ran toward us. He and Enrico chattered back and forth in Italian until Enrico finally turned to Mom. "Can you please describe your mother's ring of the wedding?' He pointed to his empty ring finger.

Mom stared at his finger, eyes at half-mast. Did she not get the question?

"She had a big-ass diamond," I chimed in. "The ring part was gold, shaped like vines, with two bands connected together. Oh, and a little diamond off to the side. Did you find it? *Che cosa ha detto?"*

"He doesn't want you to think he stole it," said Enrico. "They were cleaning the tuna—" Salvatore held up a little blue plastic bag.

"Oh, for God's sake. You've got to be kidding." Mom came to life with the snap of a rattler and grabbed at the plastic bag. Fortunately for me, I'd watched so many episodes of CSI that I knew what was coming. Mom didn't. She opened the bag and, once she realized what it contained, practically melted right into the dock. Enrico caught her before she slid into the water like one of those clocks in a Salvador Dali painting. I reached for the plastic baggy and confirmed that it was, in fact, my Grandma's ring—still encircling her aged, gray, and partly digested finger. The opalescent fingernail polish barely had a scratch.

"Holy shit," said Pen when she peeked inside the bag.

"This is why Neptune, he send the tuna to them," said Enrico. "So they can tell you your momma, she rest now with the *spirito."*

Maybe I was losing it, but I swear to this day I heard Grams whisper her favorite line in my ear. "Well, things could be worse."

How so, Grams? How so? I wondered. Then I thought back to the memory care unit at Grace Jail and I knew.

The next morning, as we packed our bags to leave the island, I slipped a little homemade *lamella* into my pocket. I asked the gardener working outside the hotel if I could have some clippings of myrtle and bougainvillea. He smiled and nodded, so I wove them into a wreath for Grams and secured it with a piece of string. Mom and I bought a little pot, hand-painted with the traditional island lemon design. I think it was meant for sugar or jam, but I eased the finger and *lamella* inside and covered them with pebbles and sand.

I taped the pot shut and put it in a sock and then into my backpack. The hotel clerk knew us by now, and gave us each cheek kisses as we checked out. We left most of Grams's things for charity, and the rest we packed into our own overstuffed bags. We bumped up the stone road, took the funicular one last time, and boarded the ferry. Pen and Salvatore said good-bye on the dock while Mom and I found seats. As we settled in, Mom reached for my hand. It was weird and awkward at first, since we had barely touched in over a year. But her hand was soft and warm like Grams's hands had been. I leaned in, and Mom brushed a stray bang away from my cheek.

"Answer me a question?" I said.

"Sure, what is it?" Mom was mellower than she'd been in about a hundred years.

"Why is our middle name Bishop?" I knew mine was because Mom's was, but I wondered if she knew why Grams had given the name to her.

Mom shrugged. "Your Grams and Grandpa Chuck always said it was a special family name. I liked it because it sounds regal. Bernadette Bishop."

She would. "How come you didn't name me after my dad?"

"People who disappear from the scene have no right to have a child named for them." Mom looked out the ferry window.

"What if they didn't mean to, disappear that is?"

Pen arrived just as Mom was about to answer. "What a dream," Pen said, as she plopped into her seat. "That guy is so fine."

Mom and I glanced at each other, eyebrows raised. I bet we were thinking the same thing: Salvatore probably had a girl on every boat. But we smiled at Pen's bliss.

When the ferry was about a mile out, the three of us headed for the outer deck. Pen held the wreath while I fished the little lemon-covered pot out of my backpack.

I pressed the pot against my cheek, kissed it, and handed it to Mom. "Here Mom, you do it."

Despite the breeze clawing at her short, chic hair, Mom cupped the finger pot in her hands, closed her eyes, and kissed it. "I miss you more than I ever imagined possible," she whispered.

"Knowing your grandma made me a better person," said Pen. "She was one of the only grown-ups who ever really gave a shit about what was happening in my life." Tears streamed down her face.

My throat ached with all the things I wanted to say but couldn't.

We leaned against the rail, Mom cradling the jar, Pen handing me the wreath. Bougainvillea thorns, hiding beneath beautiful peachy-pink flowers, pricked my fingers. I wondered where Mom's and my tears were, then smiled when I realized we were just like Grams—stoic in the face of grief. It felt right to see Mom hurl the jar into the water, lemon designs slowly turning round and round as it arced into the sea. We each touched the wreath and fingered the papery flowers before I spun it Frisbee style toward the gentle swells.

Maybe it was the sun on the water, maybe it was the weird rush of hope flooding back into my veins, but I swear I saw young Grams and Bish waving as we passed a tiny island jutting from the middle of the sea.

I touched Grams's wedding ring, which was now on my finger for safekeeping. Mom had been too grossed out by where it had been to even touch it. But to me, its journey gave it even more magical power. "Mission complete." Bish would have written in his diary. "Target 100 percent." Yet, every mission, Bish had explained, had its costs. I finally understood what he meant. I felt the pain of losing Grams, the frustration of her lingering secrets, but also the joy of having helped her live and die on her own terms, in her own way.

The salt air caught in my throat and I coughed. Tears tried to escape, but I battled them back. For once Mom didn't say a word, just put her arms around Pen and me, standing at the deck rail, stroking our hair, quietly watching Capri disappear. In that moment, none of us Bishop-Stevens girls were what the others had always believed them to be. Grams was a million miles away from complacent, Mom was amazingly vulnerable, and me—I was tougher than I thought. If there is such a thing as an old soul, I would have bet mine was as ancient as the Faraglioni Rocks of Capri. At least it felt that way.

CHAPTER TWENTY-SIX

THE LAST LETTERS

It came as no surprise that Mom wanted me to go back to Grace Retirement to pack up Grams's stuff while she made one last stop on her speaking tour. Kate too, was tied up with the early birth of her new twin boys. Even Pen had to go back to school.

Flying solo, I shouldn't have been surprised by how weirdly deserted it felt the first time I entered Grams's apartment. There was a dirty dish in the sink, a pair of shoes by the door, a FedEx letter and junk mail piled on the table. I dropped the stack of boxes I'd carried in and poked around through the mail on the desk. Out of habit, I dropped the junk mail into the garbage can as I straightened up the table. Next, I pulled the tab on the FedEx letter. There was a paper-clipped note inside, typed up and signed.

> *Dear Mrs. Stevens:*
>
> *Enclosed please find a check for the residual from the sale of your home. Your husband always meant well, and I'm sorry we had to take the foreclosure measures we did. In the end, it was for the best.*
>
> *Wishing you well in this time of loss,*
> *Dr. William Klokz*

The check was one of those big ones used by businesses. It was light green, and I blinked when I looked at the amount. Fifty-three thousand bucks. I had no way of knowing whether Grams knew this was coming. Maybe it explained why she had no problem paying for so many things on our trip. Maybe she didn't care about racking up her credit card because she knew she wasn't coming back. I bit my lip, trying not to think about all the little clues Grams had dropped that I had been too dense to notice. I dug a little deeper into the pile on the table and found a hand-scribbled letter on a yellow lined notepad. It was addressed to me.

July 14, 2003

Dear Sylvie,

  I'm writing this in a clear moment "just in case" and giving a copy to my lawyer Mr. McPherson. I know he will get it to you when it is time.

  I've often wished I had a crystal ball to see into the future, but as I've grown older, I'm glad I don't. All I can do is hope the seeds I've planted will grow even if I'm not here to tend them.

  Speaking of seeds, please don't be angry, but I took the liberty of sending an application and some samples of your artwork to the school I'd always dreamed of attending—the Art Institute of Chicago. I have no idea about their acceptance policies, but no matter what happens, anything I have left after my death will go to you for college—your choice of college. I don't want Grace Jail to take it all.

  My hope for you is that you'll follow your heart more than I followed mine. Use your fierce will and embrace your delightful imagination. Believe in the goodness of all people, be tolerant of mistakes (we all make them), and most of all do the right thing. I can give you this advice because a) I'm your grandmother, and b) by the time you read this, I'll be dead—at least to this world. Please remember me, and know I had to leave before I could no longer remember you.

Much love now and always, your
Grams (Merrilee Stevens)

The note knocked me flat into Grandpa Chuck's old designer recliner. A lump grew in my throat, and my nose ran as I tried to hold back a river of tears. They roared out of me anyway.

"Why did you have to die, Grams?" I sputtered into the quiet air. "Why did you leave me?" It seemed stupid to ask these questions when I already knew the answers. But here in Grams's cushy prison cell, the reality of her being dead sunk in. Every dark corner was a reminder of Death, lurking. Every handwritten note a last treasure. "Oh, Grams, I miss you so much."

"Quiet, Sylvie dear, you'll wake the warden."

I wiped away the tears and saw a young, dark-haired girl in a retro polka-dot swimsuit. "Grams?"

She nodded. "Isn't this marvelous? Not only can I be any physical age I like, I can remember everything." She opened her arms wide, then wrapped them around herself.

"Did you come here because I called to you?"

Grams grinned. "I was able to come here because you called me. But the truth is, I need your help. There's a letter in my old secretary desk that I need you to give to your mother. I'd forgotten about it, but she deserves to know the truth."

I blew my nose and went to the old desk made of dark golden wood. Grams had let me play secretary there a million times. I twisted the old-fashioned skeleton key that was still in its lock and lowered the wooden front. A maze of cubbyholes faced me. Some had tiny wooden figurines perched in them, others contained old-looking papers and envelopes. When I turned to ask Grams about the letter, she was gone.

"Wait!" I said, but there was no answer. Fighting back disappointment, I thumbed through the cubbies and pulled open a drawer. Inside, under a stack of old birthday cards, I found a yellowed envelope addressed to Keith Bishop, 12th Army Air Corps. It had been stamped "undeliverable" and "return to sender" with dates in June of 1945.

When I opened it, I saw why Grams so wanted me to deliver it to Mom.

April 29, 1945

My Dearest Bish,

 I'm sorry I've been silent for so long, but so much has happened here. I haven't been able to tell you because Father is so furious. You deserve to know, though, that I've given birth to a beautiful daughter, your daughter, and have named her Bernadette....

As I sat there with Grams's letter in my hand, I realized that all this time, I thought my story would start when these other stories stopped, when all the secrets were revealed — Grandpa Chuck's, Grams's, Bish's, Mom's. But the truth is, our stories are perpetual motion, totally intertwined with the stories of others. They don't even begin and end with birth and death, they go on. In photos, in bits of

paper, through words written on a page. These memories are not only
our ghosts, they are seeds of ourselves, waiting for the right conditions
to germinate. I know now that I am all of these stories, and yet my
story has just begun.

THE END

ACKNOWLEDGEMENTS

I have many people to thank for their support and assistance through the long process of writing and researching *The Tail Gunner*. First, I must thank my father, Keith Bishop Lile, for the pictures, diary, and inspiration he left behind. Although this is a work of fiction, much of it is based on his experiences during World War II. He served 59 missions between 1944 and the end of the war in 1945 and, unlike Bish, lived to talk about it. In truth, he never said much about the war and never seemed to want to, so finding this collection after his death in 1993 was a true surprise. From it, and with the help of many, I was able to piece together where he was and when, as well as some elements of his wartime life while stationed on Corsica and in Northern Italy.

For that research assistance, I am beholden to many. The folks at the 57th Bomb Wing Association were amazing, especially John Fitzgerald, Barbara Ennis Connolly, Agostino Alberti, Dominique Taddei, Charles Dills, Mick Becchi, VJ White, and the late Norm Doe. The documents and insights they shared were priceless. Additionally, Harriette Coret, Judith Berson Levinson, and Anthony Atwood deserve many thanks for providing information about basic training in Miami Beach, as does Leon Stewart with Warbirds Unlimited for sharing his knowledge of B-25s.

I am extremely grateful to my friend and tour guide Hannah Jay, who traveled though Italy with me, helping find the obscure places captured in Dad's photographs.

I also thank my tough and wonderful mentors at the Northwest Institute of Literary Arts, Carmen Bernier-Grand, Wayne Ude, Bonny Becker, and Bruce Holland Rogers, for their critical eyes and evaluation in the name of art and craft. To my friends and fellow writers Anjali Bannerjee, Claire Gebben, Charlotte Morganti, and Nancy Ackerman, I raise a glass in thanks for their support. And certainly I must thank my family, particularly my niece and nephews Haley, Krister, and Dylan, who were brave enough to go flying in a B-25 with me and who prodded me to keep on writing and digging into the story of their grandfather. I especially thank my sister Kathy, who was there with me at the burn pile in the pasture when we found and saved Dad's priceless stash.

As the first book published by Bering Street Studio, *The Tail Gunner* would not exist without its amazing crew. Thanks to these intrepid supporters this ship has taken flight: Kobbie Alamo, Steve Alexander, Viviane Arlotto, Stephanie Barbé Hammer, Phyllis Bartling, Bonny Becker, Kitty Bickford, Joanne Breidenstein, Janet Buttenwieser, Brenda Carver, Tanya Chernov, Diane DeAutremont, Yvonne Dymerski, Chris Erlich, Stefanie Freele, Claire Gebben, Donna Goggin, Iris Graville, Dylan Hall, Kathy Hall, Keegan Hall, Riley Hall, Kathy Hiles, Jackie Haskins, Bruce Holland Rogers, Guy Hoppen, John Humphrey, Tiffany Jay, Grier Jewell, Tom Krage, Barbara Lile-Duzsik, Haley Lile, Jennifer Lile, Kimberli Lile, Krister Lile, Lana Lile, Kim Lundstrom, Deborah N, Genevieve Nine, Nancy Norton, Penny and Charlie Odess, Garry Schalliol, Wayne Ude, Dimitri Van Roy, Cynthia Waldman, Sheila Ward, Steve White, Kirsten Williams, and many others who prefer the cloak of anonymity.

Lastly, and most lovingly, I thank my late fiancé, Andrei Bazdyrev, and his daughter, Juliana, for supporting me through many hours of writing and rewriting. Without their encouragement and understanding, this book would never have been completed.

Many scenes and details in *The Tail Gunner* are based on real events and circumstances encountered and documented by various people during World War II. Strafing, the bombing of rail lines, and attacks on supply stations were a very real occurrence. The strategic bombing effort that targeted rail lines along Brenner Pass was nicknamed "Operation Bingo" and was designed to disable the movement of food and goods into German-occupied Austria to help end the war in Europe.

— S.T. Lile

Flexible Gunnery School Ft. Mye
Instruction
ENGLISH-ITALI
PHRASE BOOK
COMPLIMENTS OF
THE AMERICAN NATIONAL RED CROSS
D EASTER